ALMOST FREE

LISA HELEN GRAY

Zara, Believe — Lisa x

Copyrights reserved © Lisa Helen Gray

Edited by Stephanie Farrant at Bookworm Editing Services
Cover Design by Cassy Roop at Pink Ink Designs
Paperback Interior Format by Abigail Davies at Pink Elephant Designs

No part of this publication may be reproduced or transmitted in any form or by any means, electronic or mechanical, including photocopy, recording, or any information storage and retrieval system without the prior written consent from the publisher, except in the instance of quotes for reviews. No part of this book may be scanned, uploaded, or distributed via the Internet without the publisher's permission and is a violation of the international copyright law, which subjects the violator to severe fines and imprisonment.

This book is licensed for your enjoyment. E-book copies may not be resold or given away to other people. If you would like to share with a friend, please buy an extra copy. Thank you for respecting the author's work.

This is a work of fiction. Any names, characters, places and events are all product of the author's imagination. Any resemblance to actual persons, living or dead, business or establishments is purely coincidental.

I am no longer surviving; I am living.

Prologue

Dear Lara,

I'm *almost* free.
I know the last time I wrote to you I was in a really bad place, but I promise, I'm trying really hard to move on with my life. I am.
I still feel like I'm locked in my own personal prison, surrounded by the same four walls. But those walls, Lara, they continue to make me feel safe. I know them, have memorised them, and I love the comfort they bring me. Yet lately, they're no longer the same.
I'm starting to believe those four walls are what are keeping me from moving forward. I know if you were here you'd be sitting next to me, trying to cheer me up, and if you were here, it would work. But you're not here, Lara. I don't even feel you in our room anymore. It's like you're completely gone, or maybe it's because I've started to open my eyes. I don't know.
After I found you lying in your own vomit, no longer breathing, my world changed. My life altered in a way I can never explain. Not really. Not when my problems seem insignificant compared to you no longer being in this world. I feel like I'm being selfish, unfair, but it's hard when all I have is Mum and Dad bringing me down.
I'm not you.
I'll never be you.
But more than that, I'll never be *me* again.
I don't know who I am anymore, Lara. I've lost her, and every time I try to dig deep enough to find her, I can't breathe.
I'm broken.
I've become someone else.

Someone I don't recognise.

Depression hasn't just changed me; it's changed everything. It's changed my views on life. Nothing is the same anymore. It's jaded, broken, and depressing.

It's not that I'm unhappy—although I am—it's more. I wish I was just unhappy; I could change that. I'd have the control I need to work towards the life I want, the life I had. But that isn't the case. Not with me. I feel numb all the time. I no longer care if I wake up in the morning, no longer care much about anything. It's like someone has seized every emotion from my body. I'm like a human robot.

It's exhausting.

It's weakened me, mind, body and soul. Hell, a month ago it took everything I had in me just to shower.

I hate feeling like this. I do. Depression is a gut-wrenching, soul-crushing disease which leaves you wide open and exposed. It changes you in ways you don't even realise. You stop caring, the process slow, until gradually, you don't even cry at those sad TV ads anymore. You die a little inside each day. Everything you once loved, you no longer have any feelings for. All the small things you enjoyed in life, slowly disappear over time.

Even after those changes, it could take weeks, if not months, to notice them because you're blind to it, swallowed by the heartaching numbness.

It's been over a year since I lost you—lost Lake. A year since I was attacked. I should be better by now. I should be doing something, anything, with my life. But instead, I'm still sitting in my bedroom, day in, day out, listening to Mum and Dad just tear me down further.

I swear to you, I tried. I really did. At first, I thought they were being protective, not wanting anything to happen to me, not wanting to lose another daughter. But I wasn't even close. They do nothing but tell me how worthless I am, how I'm not you and I'll never be you.

And I know I'll never be you. No one could ever be you.
I miss you, and I wish you were here. They always listened to you. I can't breathe with them down my neck constantly, their poison taking root and spreading through my body like wildfire.
It's why I've decided to change my life, to get out from under their roof and away from their cruel words. I know you'd want this for me. I just wish you could be by my side as I do it.
I do have some good news to share, though.
Lake came to see me. I know, I know, I thought she was gone, but she came back. She tried to see me, but Mum and Dad sent her away, blaming my attack on her, which was so not cool. It's one thing for them to be mean to me, but to Lake? Nuh-uh.
So anyway, I snuck out of my window early one morning and met her. We spoke about everything we missed, and I didn't blame her for leaving me. I understood.
It was great seeing her again, Lara. I even smiled. I smiled so wide and cried so hard I thought my face might crack. It felt good. I felt alive again. But I knew the minute she left to go home that the numbness would work its way in again, just like it does every time Banner leaves me. Which is why I decided right there and then, I was going to leave and attend uni.
I'm petrified and scared of what this big change will do to me mentally, but more importantly, I'm worried I'll still be the same broken girl I am inside.
I know moving won't make my problems disappear, but I am hoping it cracks that hard shell of a wall around me. Some people may be able to deal with change, no matter how big or small, and live day to day; some even out of a suitcase, moving wherever the mood takes them. I also know I'll never be that person. But I need to do it, and I've not wanted or needed anything in over a year.
The feeling is strange, but I'm pushing past it and moving forward. I guess I just wanted you to know I'm not leaving you behind or forgetting you. You'll always be in my heart, my life,

my mind. How could you not? You were the best sister anyone could ever wish for.

I love you, and I promise to write again soon.

Yours always,

Emma.

Chapter 1

Prom Night

Two Years Ago

It's finally the end of school year, the end of a gruelling two weeks of final exams, and some of the students are throwing a party to celebrate.

A few weeks ago, I had been excited about it, had planned for a night filled with laughter and fun.

But ever since my sister died from overdosing on tainted drugs, my life has been void of any joy, of anything other than a roaring darkness threatening to swallow me whole, and a need for answers.

For the past few weeks, I've focussed all my attention on finding out who sold her those drugs, denying my grief any outlet.

After many sleepless nights, all my time spent on my hunt, I found the proof I needed. I'd watched as Darren, my best friend's boyfriend, sold drugs to her brother—and made sure to get it on camera.

I'd sent her the picture, did my part as a friend, and now I'm ready to go to the police.

But it seemed fate had other plans when Warren climbed onto the roof of Banner's house.

"Hey, Emma, Luke's looking for you. He's in the kitchen," Harry, Luke's best friend, asks.

"Okay, thanks," I tell him, glancing at Warren one last time before heading back inside the house.

Banner's house is huge. His parents are lawyers or doctors or something. I'm not sure. Even though we hang out in the same crowd, we've never been close. But whatever it is they do, they must get paid well. I'm surprised they've let him have a party. Everything seems expensive. Even the kitchen table is made from thick marble and is surrounded by cream, leather chairs.

With the kids in our school, something in here is bound to get broken or Stained, with the amount of alcohol flowing.

I find my boyfriend, swaying on his feet next to the fridge, and inwardly groan. We've been going out with each other for six months, and in that time, he's done nothing but annoy me. Before I agreed to go out with him, he seemed so well put together, smart, and fun. Now he's a slobbering idiot who acts like a two-year-old when he's had a sip of beer.

I'm ready to turn around and leave, but he sees me. "Emma! We have to talk."

"I'm busy, Luke, can't this wait? I'm meeting Lake outside."

He staggers his way over to me, his eyes glazed over. "You know, I tried to be your boyfriend, your friend, but you're making it hard. It's been weeks since you lost your sister; you need to move on," he slurs.

My blood runs cold at the mention of my sister. And even though he's highly intoxicated right now, he means every word. It's been a long time coming.

"What?" I whisper, too appalled at his behaviour. "Why would you say that? She was my sister, Luke. I can't just move on."

"Whatever," he grunts, waving his hand at me. "What I'm trying to say is I'm sleeping with Laurie Price. She pays me attention, gets me."

I glance away, no longer able to look at him without feeling sick. I'm not hurt he's cheated; I'm relieved. The only reason I've held on for so long is because I needed some sort of attachment to my old life, to the me before my sister died. I'm also pissed, because he could have told me another way, not drunk and in a room full of people.

"Okay," I say, not willing to show him any kind of emotion, and turn to walk away. He laughs, and my spine stiffens with the condescension in his tone, but I pivot to face him once more. "What?"

"You're such a bitch," he yells, gaining everyone in the kitchen's attention. I look through the crowd of faces, friends from school, and blink back tears at the whispers, the stares. I had enough of it when my sister died.

"You've had a lot to drink, Luke. I'll talk to you when you're sober."

"That's it, walk away," he shouts, throwing his arms out wide. "I break up with you, and you don't care. I tell you I'm cheating on you, and you don't even blink."

I clench my hands into fists. "You know what? We're done—so fucking done."

I don't stand around to listen to him shout abuse at me. Instead, I rush out the room, towards the back garden. I knock into a hard body, and arms reach out to steady me. I glance up through blurry vision to see Banner looking down at me with his deep hazel eyes.

"I'm sorry."

"Are you okay?"

I nod, shoving out of his grip, and exit through the patio doors. A few people are milling around, but a sudden shouting match at the front of the house has them leaving to investigate.

I furiously wipe at my cheeks, hating myself for being so weak. I should be happy I finally found out who sold the drugs to my sister. Drugs that killed her.

But all I feel is empty.

The lone stone bench under a large tree looks inviting, secluded, even though it's still close to the house. I walk over and sit down, dropping my head into my hands, breathing in and out slowly.

The night air is still, chilly, but it's good to feel something—anything.

"What the fuck did you say?" I hear roared into the darkness, and spin around to find Darren—the guy who killed my sister—storming towards me from the side of the house with angry strides.

She may have taken the drugs, but he's the one who tempted her, the reason she was around them in the first place. I don't know whether she was hooked—I couldn't bear to read any more of her diary—but I do know he tempted her, made many promises and told her they were safe. She only mentioned taking them once in the diary, and she also wrote about being in love with the person who sold them to her, writing about how he understood her. He was also the one who broke her heart when she discovered he had a girlfriend, despite being in a relationship with her. It wasn't until tonight that I found out it was Darren.

"Stay the fuck away from me, Darren. Your secret's out. I've already sent the photo to the police, and to Lake. You're a fucking murderer," I scream, getting up.

He reaches for me, and while before I hadn't been paying attention, too lost in the hollowness trying to consume me, he's got all my focus now.

The fury in his face has me stepping back, but I'm too late. He grabs my arm in a tight grip, pulling me roughly towards him. His pupils are huge, and so black he looks demonic.

"I've lost Lake because of you. She won't even talk to me. She thinks I'm a murderer. You and your fucking crazy theories. You need to keep your mouth fucking shut."

I bite back a grimace of pain. "Never!"

He shakes me like a ragdoll, before pushing with such force my feet lift from the ground and I fly backwards, landing on the grass with a grunt.

I look up at him, horrified. He's always been a bit of an arsehole, but I never thought he'd be capable of this.

"You need to delete that picture," he tells me, walking over to where I lie on the ground. I shrink back as he comes closer and lean up on my hands.

"Darren, you need to pay for what you did," I bite out, struggling not scream at him and make him angrier. I also don't take my eyes off him, not trusting him for a second.

He screams, sounding like an animal in pain. I flinch, trying to slap his hands away when he reaches for me.

A sharp pain to my leg has me crying out, giving him the opportunity to grab me. My scalp feels like it's on fire as he grasps a chunk of my hair and drags me further into the darkness of the garden, no longer in sight of the house, the scent of roses and freshly cut grass so at odds with my pain and fear.

I panic, my fingers digging into his wrists, hoping he'll loosen his grip or let me go all together.

"Darren, what are you doing?" I cry out.

"Are you going to tell them you lied?" he asks, dropping me to the ground.

I wince, lifting a hand to my sore scalp. I look up at him, angry he would ask this of me. "You killed my sister. Did you really think I'd let you get away with it? I read her diary, you know. I know all about your cheating on Lake, and so does she," I tell him, glaring.

"You little fucking slut," he screams, pulling at his hair.

I try to get up, but his eyes shoot to me, looking crazed and dark. Like a footballer booting a ball into its goal, he kicks me. He kicks me with such force I roll over, winded and in shock.

I get up on all fours, needing to get out of here, but before I can move, hands pull me back by my dress. I hear a seam rip, the dress loosening from my body. And as I roll over, trying to hide my bare skin, I feel a different kind of fear snake through me.

His eyes meet mine, and I don't recognise him—see any glimmer of the lad I grew up with.

He screams, sounding so crazed, I fear for my life. He doesn't sound human. I feel paralysed, which is why when he kneels over me, his fists hitting me in every place possible, all I can do is shriek my pain into the night. Every punch feels like torture, like someone's stabbing me with a hot poker.

When darkness begins to pulse around the edges of my vision, I close my eyes, no longer crying out as he lands blow after blow to my body.

"Hey, what's going on back here? The party's over; you need to go home."

Banner.

I try to blink my eyes open, but they won't obey my silent command, my eyelids feeling swollen. I'm cold, and I can no longer feel the dress on my body.

"What the fuck?" Banner roars, and the weight of Darren on top of me, pressing me down into the grass and mud, is suddenly lifted.

My head rolls to the side, and through tiny slits, I watch as Banner punches Darren over and over.

What seems like hours later, I feel something warm cover my

body, the scent of aftershave, strong with a mix of spices, making me feel safe.

A warm hand lifts mine from the cold, damp ground and grips it gently, as if afraid anything more will hurt me.

"Emma, it's Banner. It's going to be fine. I've called for an ambulance and the police are on their way," he says gently in my ear.

My heart wants to believe him, it truly does, but as I lay on the frigid grass, shivers racking through me, I know nothing will e ver be the same again.

Chapter 2

I don't even recognise the girl staring back at me in the mirror. Two weeks ago, my cheekbones had stood out in stark relief; my thick, brown hair had hung limp down my back, the strands the texture of straw; and my eyes had been swollen, dull and tired, with dark circles beneath. I had been weak, my body near skeletal.

Now, my cheeks have filled out, a healthy pink tinge to them. My hair is shiny and sleek, and my blue eyes, looking more green today, are sparkling with life—something I haven't felt in a long time.

Months ago, I decided to move out of my parent's house, away from their malicious and cruel words.

I was suffering with depression, not only from being attacked, but from losing my sister. Finding her body after she had overdosed became my undoing. I changed that day, not only after finding her but... from having to live without her. She was the cheese to my toast, the sausage to my mash. She was everything to me—even if in the last few months of her life she had become distant. She had been older than me, but not by much, since my parents had me eleven months after Lara.

My parents had loved her more. A lot more. It never bothered me because I had my friends; I had my grandparents who loved and adored me.

After she died, my parents made sure to let me know every chance they got that they wished it had been me. It didn't matter that Lara took drugs of her own free will, only that it wasn't me who had died.

I hated them—I still do. All my life I had tried to get them to love me, but I was a mistake, something they never planned for or wanted —and couldn't get rid of.

For two years their damning words ate away at me, leaving me a shell of the person I once was.

But then, one day, I got news that my best friend, Lake, was alive. She hadn't died, like I always feared, but ran away, escaping the accident she thought she caused. She's happy now, with a new family as well as back with her own. And is even in love.

From that day, I built myself up the best I could to give me the strength to leave the house. I went to my psychiatrist every week and started taking medicine.

With the help of my grandparents, my cousin, and the money I made from self-publishing books, I was able to move out.

The only thing my parents hated about me leaving was that I was taking their person to blame for their favourite daughter's death away from them. They screamed, shouted, made sure to tell me until they were blue in the face that I'd be back, but would never be welcome.

I wouldn't.

I'd never go back.

They helped destroy the girl I once was, but with months of intense therapy, I've finally managed to say goodbye to her and welcome the new me.

I still have a way to go before I'm fully recovered. I still suffer with insomnia, and when I do manage to sleep, I have nightmares, from the night my sister died to the night I was attacked by my best friend's boyfriend.

Another person who has been huge help in my recovery is Banner. George Banner. Though we never really spoke in school, since the night I was attacked by Darren, we've become really close. I couldn't have got through everything if he hadn't been there, supporting me every step of the way.

He saved me, not only from Darren, but from myself.

He would sneak through my bedroom window and talk to me about everything and anything, not caring if I contributed to the conversations or not. Sometimes, he would just sit with me, both of us silent, just to make sure I never felt alone.

I'd be so lost in grief I couldn't see the light at the end of the tunnel. It wasn't until he went off to college that I realised how I'd come to rely on his visits, how they would keep me chained to reality.

Now, I'm living with my cousin, Mark, and his boyfriend, Levi. I haven't met Levi in person yet, but I have spoken to him during one of my many Facetime chats with Mark.

Both are still away on holiday for another week, which leaves me alone in this tiny flat. I also won't see Banner for another couple of days as he's travelling with his football team for a match against another college.

Despite being close—so close it feels like losing a limb when he's not around—our relationship has never extended beyond friendship. But recently, my feelings towards him have changed. My heart pounds whenever he's close, and I find myself wanting to touch him, to know what his lips feel like. And it's growing more powerful with every passing moment. It's hard not to want him when he's everything a girl could want in boy.

Shaking my thoughts from my mind, I finish throwing my hair up in a messy bun before making my way outside.

My hands tremble as soon as the door clicks shut behind me, but I clench them into fists, refusing any trepidation an outlet, knowing I can't revert to my old ways, when I was too scared to leave the house, too afraid of what people would say or do. I couldn't take the condolences any longer. I couldn't take another pitiful look passed my way. I can't be that person anymore—I refuse to.

But being here is a fresh start for me.

It didn't help that I was scared of my own shadow, afraid of what would happen to me next. Bad luck comes in threes, and already I had lost my sister and got attacked by someone I never really saw as a threat—just a dickhead.

Life had a way of changing, though. Now, I was attending late-night classes at Whithall University, which is a massive step for me. The thought of being around so many people during daytime classes is enough to break me out in hives. Maybe in time I will get there, but at the moment, I just want to take things slowly, to catch my breath.

I'm still not a people person, and I don't think I ever will be, but I can only take one step at a time. I've taken the first step by moving out of my parent's toxic home. Now I'm moving onto the second:

University.

Jordan, a girl referred to me by the college to show me around, meets me outside our building. It's drizzling with rain, the night sky filled with dark clouds, not a single star in sight.

She's scary beautiful; she has a Mylee Cyrus/ Kelly Osbourne thing going on. Her hair is cut into a bob, the ends pink on one side and the other shaved to the scalp.

My gaze drifts over her tattoos and piercings, already liking her from the image alone. She doesn't dress or style for anyone other than herself. She looks fierce, and if I had to guess, I'd say she has a fierce personality, too.

She steps away from the lamppost she was leaning against, smiling. "Hey, I'm Jordan, we spoke on the phone. It's nice to meet you."

"Hi." I wave, feeling a tad nervous. I glance around, ignoring the rising panic in my chest. If I don't do this now, I'll never do it. My mind will tell me I'm too scared, when in fact, I'm just a nervous mess. I need to remind myself nothing is going to happen. "Thank you again for doing this. I bet you have better things to do than babysit me."

She waves me off. "It's fine, I don't mind—and I offered. Mr. Hanna said you were taking a few classes to improve your writing skills?"

"I am," I tell her, not explaining further. I took some online classes when I was back home, but that's it. I'm not about to tell her I'm an indie author who writes under a pen name. I'd rather stay anonymous for as long as I possibly can. Only Banner, my grandparents, and Mark know I write books, just not which ones. I'm not confident enough in my ability for them to read them, even if Banner hounds me relentlessly for the titles.

"How long have you lived here?" she asks as we begin to walk.

I glance over at Jordan, smiling. "Only a few weeks. I moved in with my cousin, Mark, and his boyfriend, Levi. But they're away on holiday at the moment. It's why I signed up for a tour guide. Mark was going to show me around, but I thought I'd get it out of the way while I had nothing else to do."

"I can understand that. I got lost so many times when I first came here, but luckily for you, you're only sectioned in one building. We should be able to meet Mr. Flint, your Historical Literature teacher, and Mr. Hanna, your teacher for English Literature. I don't know Mr. Flint—I've never taken one of his classes—but Mr. Hanna is a brilliant teacher. I had him last year."

"Did you enjoy it? I hear it's hard."

She seems to mull that over, tilting her head from side to side. "Um, not really, but I understood it. Most people take the course to learn a new language, not to improve on one they already know. But he is a good teacher and I've not heard anyone moan over him being unfair."

"What are you hoping to do with your degree?" I ask, as there are a million and one things you can do with an English major.

"I'm a blogger at the moment. I run a blog called Whithall Scandals, but after, I'd like to maybe teach or write. I'm not sure yet. I've still got time before I have to decide, anyway."

"Whithall Scandals," I murmur, wondering where I've heard that name before. When it comes to me, my head snaps in her direction and my eyes widen. "Oh, my Gosh, you're the one who helped all those girls, aren't you?"

She flinches, and I inwardly kick myself for my lack of social skills. "Yeah. It's been a rough time here, but I promise everything is okay now."

"Wasn't there a murder a few weeks back?" I ask dubiously.

She chuckles, running her fingers through her hair. "You're right. It sucks it happened, but as far as we know, it was a one-time incident. We do have protocols here to keep us safe, and they are encouraging students to abide by them."

"What, like the buddy system?" I ask, remembering how my friend, Lake, and I would go to the toilet together at parties.

"Yeah. I'm sorry. I'm not really doing a good job, am I—to help make you feel safe?"

I'm startled by her comment, not knowing what she means. The thought of her knowing about my past is enough to send bile to the back of my throat. "It's fine. You're only telling me the truth, and I appreciate that. I know now to be more vigilant."

She gives me a warm smile and I relax. "Thank you. If you do ever need someone to come with you somewhere, you have my email and phone number. Just message or call me."

"I will, thank you."

"Okay, this is the English building," she says, gesturing to the huge, old, stone building in front of us. We're in a courtyard, wooden benches scattered here and there, and tall, neatly trimmed hornbeam trees travelling the circumference. "That entrance will take you to Mr. Hanna's classroom, and this one leads you to Mr. Flint's," she tells me, leading me over to the door she explained Mr. Flint's classroom would be at.

There's a few cleaners in the halls, polishing the floor, but other than that, it's quiet. It's kind of creepy. I shiver, running my hands up and down my arms.

"This place is giving me chills," I whisper.

She laughs, and the sound echoes down the hall. "It is. I've never liked this building. It's one of the older ones. The library, if you ever need to use it, is just on the other side of this one. If you turn left at the path instead of walking straight ahead to come here, it will lead you right to it."

"I'll have to remember that. I want to check it out. My cousin said they have a really good collection of classics."

"They do. My friend works there. There's also a section of books you can't check out due to them being first editions, but she's cool and lets me sneak them out. I read The Great Gatsby before moving on to some Jane Austen. I'm still going through them."

"I'm definitely going to have to check it out." I smile, excited now about going. "Can we read them in the library?"

"Yeah, you just can't check some of them out. If you want, I can introduce you to Allie. She's one of the librarians. She won't mind you taking one home as long as you promise to bring it back."

"You'd do that for me?" I ask, more excited than ever. Some of the books in the library are legendary. I looked up the history of the library, finding out it has some rare treasures inside that are locked in cases at the back.

"Yeah, of course. I know they're closed for another two days—someone broke in and made a mess of the place—but it will be open after that."

I gasp, horrified. "None of the book were ruined, were they?"

She giggles, gazing at me with amusement. "A few, but most are tech books or something boring."

"Good." I sigh, relaxing, but immediately come alert when she taps on a door with her knuckles.

A deep voice echoes from the other side. "Come in."

She pushes the door open, sticking her head through first. "Hi, Mr. Flint, I'm Jordan. I'm here to show your new student, Emma Burton, around."

"Come in, come in."

I don't know what I expected when I thought of my teacher, but it wasn't someone so young. He must be in his late twenties at the most.

He stands when we enter, a smile lighting his face as he reaches out to shake my hand. I smile, taking his hand politely, trying to slow my breathing at the contact.

I hate being touched by people I don't know. It's something I've not been able to overcome since Darren attacked me all those years ago.

"Hi, I'm Emma. I'll be starting in a week."

He doesn't let go of my hand, and my palms sweat. "It's always great to meet new students."

I pull my hand out of his grasp, using more force than I should have had to. When I look up, something in his eyes has me stepping back, nearly bumping into Jordan.

"Do you have a list of materials she'll need, and her curriculum?" Jordan asks when I'm too tongue-tied to speak.

He looks away, still smiling as he addresses her. "Of course. One moment."

I stay silent, avoiding Jordan's questioning gaze. I smile politely out of habit and take the papers he hands me. "Thank you."

"When do you start?" he asks, his smile slimy.

I think about it for a minute, knowing I start later than other students since I had to register with a new therapist. "I think next Wednesday."

"I'll look forward to seeing you."

I look away, biting my lip.

"Um, okay, we'll let you get back to your work. I just wanted to show her where her classes will be."

"It's fine. I'm always happy to be interrupted by two pretty ladies."

I watch Jordan's expression turn from relaxed and happy, to a little taken aback.

"Okay, well… bye," Jordan says slowly, and I turn, ready to get the hell out of here.

"Bye, and see you soon, Emma," he says.

I glance over my shoulder, finding him watching my arse, and flinch.

Pervert.

Having him as a teacher is going to be a bad idea. I can already feel it.

Chapter 3

I wake up screaming, my nightmare holding me in its clutches. Instead of Darren's face attacking me in my dreams, I see Mr. Flint, my new teacher.

I sit up, wiping my sweaty, clinging hair from my face. I run a hand over my face before looking up and surveying my new room.

It still saddens me there's no trace of my sister here. Only me. She was a girly girl, and I'm just a plain Jane. We were two different souls, but we were best friends.

And now she's gone.

Having the nightmare still fresh in my mind, I think back to my attack. I still don't remember much, only parts, and even then, they are blurred.

When they arrested Darren, he was charged with assault and attempted rape. He admitted to the assault, but said he had no intention of raping me, so he wasn't sentenced for it. I don't know what his intentions were. All I know is, that night I was afraid for my life. I thought I was going to die, and at one point, I woke up wishing I had.

When Banner found me, my dress had been torn off and Darren was on top of me. If he hadn't of come, I dread to think what would have happened. I was in hospital for a week, recovering from broken bones and lacerations to my face.

Shit. Banner.

I jump from my bed, flinging my drawers open and grabbing the first items I find, before heading to the bathroom.

I promised Banner we could meet up and go for breakfast. He knows about my issues and has never tried to push me to do something I didn't want to. When he sensed my reluctance, he calmed me down and promised me the place was quiet, that only the factory workers eat there.

I rush through my shower, nearly forgetting to wash out my conditioner. I've barely finished drying my hair when the door knocks. Sighing, I look in the mirror, wishing I could do something to cover up the dark circles under my eyes. Banner has seen me at my worst, so I know it doesn't faze him. I just want him to see me differently now.

I've been in love with him for a while, my feelings so strong it hurts to deny them. He's only ever been the best to me, but over time, over chats and space apart, my feelings for him grew. I just wish he felt the same way about me, but sometimes I wonder if he sticks with me because he feels sorry for me.

I run to the door, taking one last deep breath before opening it, pasting on a bright smile. "Hey, I've missed you."

He beams at me, stepping inside the flat and lifting me in one fell swoop. He spins us round and I laugh, wrapping my arms around his neck.

Yes, I've definitely missed this—missed him.

"I'm so glad you're here. I hated that you were so far away."

He puts me down gently and I look up at him, still smiling so bright I feel like my face might crack. "Well, now we're five minutes away from each other."

He grins, looking so devasting, I swoon. "Hell, yeah we are. You ready to go out for breakfast or is there some other stuff you need to do?"

My nerves are still a little bit wobbly, but with Banner, I can do anything. He makes me feel safe. "Yep. I want to hear all about football, your friends, and what you did on your break."

"Let's go, then, because I have a lot to tell you. Tom, one of the lads on my team, hooked up with this chick when we were at an away game and took her back to his room. Rafner, our other team player, is sharing a room with him, right," he says with enthusiasm. "Then, he wakes up in the morning to find Tom cuddled up to him and throws a fit. The chick he got with ended up in another player's bed—Ross—because Tom fell asleep before she finished in the bathroom or some shit. Anyway, the two of them were shit-arsed drunk, so they slept in. Coach went to see what the hold-up was, and we followed. We managed to get pictures."

"What about the chick?" I ask, stepping outside into the drizzling rain. He tucks me into his side, shielding me from the light downpour as we run to his parked car.

I close my eyes, revelling in the feel of being in his arms. It's moments like these that I cherish, because I know if he ever gets a girlfriend, I'll lose them.

He laughs, his chest vibrating against my side. "She was still with Ross outside the door and spilled the whole story. Tom had pointed her out and asked her why she wasn't the one in bed. It's why we got back early. Coach didn't want to do any stops as punishment."

He opens the car door and I step in, grateful to be out of the rain so I can hear him better. I watch him walk around the front of the car, impressed by his physique and extremely good looks. It's his eyes that captivate you to him, though, they're a deep-set hazel colour, and with his thick, dark eyebrows, they stand out like a beacon. I've never seen eyes so mesmerising. And his smilehis smile is like sunshine; it brightens up your day. I drool and melt into a puddle every single time.

It can be kind of annoying.

"What time was you meant to be back?" I ask when he drops into the driver's seat and starts up the car.

He glances over at me, smiling, before pulling out into the road. "We were due back later tonight. It's why I texted you yesterday about meeting up for breakfast."

"So, were they naked in bed together?"

He chuckles, shaking his head at me. "No, they weren't, thank god. I see enough of their junk in the showers," he tells me dryly. "When do Mark and Levi get back from their holiday?"

Banner hasn't met Mark face-to-face, but Banner has been there when Mark Facetimed me during my recovery.

"He actually texted me last night to say they were flying home tonight. Levi got food poisoning and just wants to come home."

Banner winces and pulls into a car park outside a row of factories. He points to the left, where a bunch of smaller buildings are, and says, "It's just over there. And poor fucker. I remember the time I got food poisoning. We were in Spain and I think I was thirteen-fourteen. I spent eight days out of the fifteen in bed, vomiting. I just wanted to go home, too. At least there I had my PlayStation and a television that was in English."

I giggle. "I can see you missing your video games and TV shows."

We get out of the car, meeting each other around the front. He pulls me against him again, and I glance up at his side profile, wondering if he knows how much it affects me when he does stuff like this—like we're a couple.

"My mum spoiled me for weeks after I recovered," he says, grinning down at me.

I roll my eyes because his mum spoils him, anyway. She's like no other mum I've ever met. She's cool, funny, and so loving and protective it's not even funny. His parents adore Banner and his sisters, Kacey and Louise.

"Your mum spoils you, anyway," I tell him, shoving my shoulder against his arm.

He looks down at me, smirking. "Yeah, she does."

We step inside the cute little café they built into a newer building at the side of a factory. I look around and instantly relax. He was right, the place feels safe, secure, and not too many people sitting around to make me feel uncomfortable.

He steers me over to an empty table and sits me down, taking the seat next to be as opposed to the one opposite.

"Has your mum seen your new tattoo?" I ask him, picking up the menu.

Banner is covered in tattoos. I'm surprised he found room for any more. He's had them since he was sixteen and looked old enough to get them. His mum doesn't even care, and the school only made him cover them with plasters.

He looks down at the new semicolon on his thumb. He clears his throat, glancing back up at me, something in his eyes I can't decipher. "She's the one that helped me choose it."

"She helped you choose it?" I ask, taking his hand and getting a closer look.

It just a simple, small tattoo. When we've spoken about them before, he's told me at great length how each and every one meant something to him.

"Yeah, she did."

"What made you get this one?" I ask, looking up at him through my lashes.

He blinks, looking away for a split second. "Um, for you."

I sit back, puzzled. Did he get it because I write books? That's kind of sweet. And permanent.

"For me?"

He rubs the back of his neck, shifting in his seat. "Yeah. For your story. You paused for a while before continuing your story, your life. You could have chosen to end it, but you didn't. You knew you had more to say, to give. It represents those who are brave, those who fight every day to keep living. When I asked Mum what I should get, she sent me this. I couldn't think of anything better to describe you. I've never met anyone who is as strong as you, has faced what you have and still pulled through," he says, shrugging like he hasn't just rocked my world.

I blink back tears, feeling my throat close. There were moments, many of them, where I wanted to end it all, but when I tried, my sister's face would flash behind my eyes and I couldn't. I had to live for her, for myself. She might have killed herself, but she didn't do it intentionally. She did a stupid thing and it took her life.

I glance up from the tattoo and find myself lost in the depth of his hazel eyes. I can't seem look away. He's never gotten a tattoo for me before, but he's done many things that have made me pause, take stock, and fall for him harder. Although, getting a tattoo to represent me beats everything else in comparison. It's the sweetest, most thoughtful thing to do. And kind of romantic.

I clear my throat and look away, breaking the spell he has me under. "I love it. Thank you."

"It's nothing," he says thickly.

I wonder if one day I'll ever have the courage to tell him how I feel, or if I'll be too chicken shit to lose our friendship. Knowing my luck, by the time I do find the courage, he'll be with someone else and I'll never know if he feels the same way. I'm pretty positive he doesn't, but he sends so many mixed signals, I can never tell. I used to be good at this stuff—boys. I could tell what they were thinking and if they were really into a girl or just wanted a quick lay. Now I'm so far out of my depth it's not even funny.

"So, there's something I need to"

"Banner, hey, you're back from footy."

My hands automatically go under the table and into my lap, my fingers entwining around each other with nerves. The girl walking over to us is beautiful, stunningly so. She's everything I'm not. I've not even met her and already I'm jealous. She's confident, sexy, and has more chance to get with Banner than I do.

I glance over at him to gauge his reaction. His jaw is clenched, seeming annoyed by her appearance.

"Fi, how's it going?"

She bounces to a stop at our table, and for the first time I notice the apron around her waist and notepad in hand.

"It's going great. Dad made me work today. Someone called in sick. Did you want to meet up after I finish?" she asks sweetly, batting her lashes.

I inwardly cringe, ducking down in my chair to make myself invisible.

Why now? Why when I'm with him with no choice but to witness it? It's humiliating.

"I'm sorry, Fi, but I told you: I don't any of my team's exes."

She cocks her hip to the side, her smile forced now. "Nobody likes Alec after what he did to his ex-girlfriend. No one would judge you for going out with me."

Who is Alec and why have I never heard of him? He speaks of all his team mates so I'm not sure why he's never mentioned him before.

And she's asked him out before and he's said no? But she's still trying? I don't know whether to stare in awe or embarrassment.

Awkward.

"Look, I'm gonna be straight with you. You're a sweet girl, but I'm really not interested. I'm sorry. I don't want to hurt your feelings."

Her eyes fill with tears, but she nods, her back straightening. "I can live with that. Thank you for being honest." He gives her a small smile, his eyes flicking to me and wincing. She follows his line of sight and flinches. "I'm so sorry. Are you here on a date?"

I shake my head, wanting her to calm down. She looks ready to bolt, and I need food. "No, you're fine. We're just friends."

Banner noticeably grimaces at the word, puzzling me, but I shake it off, not wanting to read too much into it.

"Oh, good. But still, I'm sorry. I get a little struck when I see hot guys. I forget about anyone else who is around. I'm truly sorry."

I smile at her bubbliness. I no longer hate her. She's actually kind of refreshing and nothing like the girl I imagined she would be. And I thought she'd be shallow, big-headed, and stuck up. I guess you really shouldn't judge a book by its cover.

"It's fine."

She inhales, putting her pen to her pad, and smiles brightly. "Right, I'm going to take your order then go cry to my dad about being rejected, then cry some more about doing it in front of a potential date. So, what can I get ya?"

I giggle a little, but it turns into a laugh when Banner turns pale.

"Let's not talk to your dad about me, okay?"

Fi turns to Banner and chuckles. "I'm joking. I'll do that stuff privately. My dad would probably come out here and thank you for not going out with me. He doesn't want me seeing boys." She pauses, seeming to think of something. "Then again, he'll probably go mad again for you not wanting to go out with me because you think there's something wrong with me. Keeping it to myself seems like a good idea."

Banner relaxes in his chair. "That would be great."

"What can I get ya?"

We both rattle off our order, then wait for her to leave before facing each other.

"Okay, who is she and who is Alec? Why don't I know about him?"

He rubs the back of his neck before resting his forearms on the table, leaning in closer. "Did you read about what happened last year, around Halloween?"

I did. I think the whole world did. Two lads from the university were raping girls and kept a record of it. When they were arrested, more girls came forward.

"Yeah, why?"

"The girl who got them arrested was best friends with one of the rapists, the one who raped her. Alec was actually going out with her when they started school. I'd met Alec before for trials and he seemed an okay lad. He cheated on her a few times—that I know of—but who am I to say something," he tells me.

I nod, trying to keep up. "Okay."

"Anyway, when she was raped, he accused her of cheating on him because of it being her best friend."

"And you don't like him because of that?"

Banner grits his teeth, leaning back in his chair. "No, I don't like him because there was a picture going around of her and he spread it. Logan, the guy who raped her, was also on our team. Not many of us liked him, and the ones that did are no longer on the team as the school couldn't prove they weren't involved too. They filed a dispute and signed a petition to get him to play, causing trouble around the campus, so in the end, they got expelled. When Alex spread that shit, and we found out it was rape, and that Logan did it, we all stopped playing until they were dropped. Logan was pulled from the team straight away until the university investigated, but Alec got away with everything."

"He's still on the team?" I ask, shocked, appalled they'd let someone like that play. Football around here is a big thing. People from all over come to watch them play. I remember when Banner first started. He got pumped because his captain got chosen to play for an actual league.

He frowns, fiddling with the salt from the table. "Yeah. We tried to get him off the team, but without proof he sent some of those messages, there was nothing we could do."

"Couldn't you show them the sent messages?"

"No. Anyone decent deleted that shit straightaway. The ones who didn't sure did after Liam Cole threatened retribution to anyone who had it."

"Who's that?"

"One of the best rugby players I've met. He's also with the girl who was raped. I heard rumours that those who didn't delete the picture found themselves with no money, their grades disappearing, and their application for housing next term declined."

I gasp, shocked and kind of impressed. Not that they didn't deserve it; they did. "He did all that for his girlfriend?"

Banner laughs. "No, his best friend, CJ, who is a computer whizz, did it. I've never actually met him, but others think he's a god. They both are. They're legendary around here."

"Impressive," I whisper, still amazed someone had the brains to do all that and get away with it.

I sit back when Fi walks over with our drinks and food, placing them down in front of us. When she leaves, I pick up my fork and face Banner.

"Has everything been sorted with that? I mean, a girl was murdered."

He winces. "I'm not sure about the murder. But Logan and Jamie were arrested."

"That's good."

He finishes chewing his food, swallowing. "Before we get sidetracked again, I wanted to ask you something."

I look up from my bacon. "Anything."

He clears his throat, pushing food around on his plate with his fork. "Since the whole Logan and Alex theatrics, Coach wants us to go on team building exercises. Our next one is unsupervised as it's voluntary. But a few of us thought it would be good to go out there with some friends and make the most of a paid getaway."

"Okay," I say, unsure of where this is going or what it has to do with me.

"I was wondering if you wanted to come with me. It's in a few months so you've got plenty of time. I just wanted to give you a heads up. I know you like to plan stuff out."

I'm not sure how good I'll be around a group of people in an enclosed space. We'd be together, whether we sleep apart or not.

"How many people are going?" I ask, not wanting to let him down.

"With us, ten. The others think the whole team building is a joke, so they decided to do something else."

Ten people. That's not so bad, and it would be stepping out of my comfort zone.

Then an idea occurs to me. "If I go, then you have to do me a favour."

He grins, and his chest puffs out. "Anything."

"Lake is coming down in a few weeks with her boyfriend to meet me. Will you come with me?"

He shakes his head at me, smiling. "I'd have done that anyway. How is she?"

I smile, thinking of our last conversation. "Happy. Her parents and brother have just moved down to be close to her."

"I've not spoken to her mum in a while. I usually check in on Warren to see how he's doing. I've not had time," he says, looking guilty.

Warren, Lake's twin brother, was in a car crash the same night I was attacked. He wasn't brain damaged, but his brain doesn't function the way it should. It made him slower, and to others he seems like he's in a kid-like state continuously, but he's not. He can still learn, still remember; he just can't do it the way we do.

He and Banner were friends before Warren started withdrawing and taking drugs. He pushed everyone away, including his sister.

I take his hand, squeezing it. "He's fine—getting married. Lake said Marybeth is beautiful."

"No way. He and Marybeth are getting married?" He grins, his face filled with happiness.

"Yep."

"Good for him. I'm happy for him."

"Maybe next time they come down she'll bring him. I know he

needs supervision, but I'm sure he'll be fine with Lake. Her boyfriend… I'm not sure. From what she's said he's a little crazy," I tell him, giggling.

"She needs that. I bet the past couple of years haven't been easy for her."

I sigh, looking down at my half-eaten food. "No, it hasn't. I'm just glad she's back. I've missed her."

"Not as much as she's missed you, I bet."

I look up, titling my head to the side. "What makes you say that?"

"Because I only came to school and I missed you. At least I got to speak to you. She didn't."

I blush, ducking my head. He always knows how to make me swoon.

"Maybe," I whisper, then clear my throat and change the subject. "Now, tell me more about your trip. I want to hear everything."

I rest my fork down, crossing my arms on the table, and listen to him talk, trying not to fantasise about his lips on mine.

When it comes to George Banner, I'm totally screwed. Because every time his mouth forms a word or puckers, a tiny sigh escapes my lips.

Chapter 4

Being away from my parents' overbearing and constant snide remarks has already made a difference in my life.

When Mark and Levi got back from holiday a week ago, I spent the first couple of days walking around on eggshells, waiting for the other shoe to drop. But they never made me feel like I was in the way, an inconvenience, or yelled at me once for getting up for a drink in the middle of the night and waking them up. The night in question, Levi actually stayed and had a cup of tea with me and chatted. He didn't scream at me for being selfish and waking him up; he didn't wish I was dead before storming off.

I think it took that moment for me to realise I wasn't going to be subject to my parents' verbal abuse again.

It felt freeing.

"Lover boy's here," Mark yells through the flat.

I groan, knowing Banner had to have heard that through the door. I hear the front door open and deep mumbling sounds start up in the living room. I dread to think what Mark is saying to him.

Not wanting Mark to embarrass me any further, I grab my coat and school bag before heading out of my room.

My room, which Mark has turned into my new favourite place. I went to my first night class last Wednesday and came back to my room having been redecorated with brand new furniture.

My grandparents had much to play in it, but it was Mark, Levi and Banner who did all the grunt work.

I have a large round chair that is so snuggly when you sink into it, I never want to leave. They know how much I hate writing at a desk. It makes me feel like my writing is a job, a chore, and not the release and hobby it's become. Knowing that, they went out and got me a chair I could lie back in. It's so huge my legs can straighten in front of me and only my feet will dangle over the edge.

It's brilliant.

Dangling from the ceiling above my bed, they've fitted different sized and coloured dreamcatchers, knowing how bad my nightmares can be. I love them and often fall asleep watching them sway.

I have a new dresser, new sheets, and other little gadgets they thought I'd love, and I do. What they did was amazing and so thoughtful I cried for a solid twenty minutes. Mark didn't know what to do, but luckily Levi and Banner had already seen it coming and got out a tub of Ben and Jerry's.

I snap back to the present when I walk into the living area, surprised to see all three ready to go out and waiting for me.

I look between them, puzzled. "Are you going out?" I ask Mark, glancing at the time. They said they were staying in and watching their soaps tonight.

"No. We're coming to dinner with you guys before you head to class."

My eyes find Banner's, silently questioning him if it's okay. He smiles. "I asked if they wanted to tag along. Hope that's okay?"

"No, he didn't," Levi grunts. "Mark wanted to spend time with you and accused Banner of occupying all of your time."

I repress the smile tugging at my lips and look to Mark, raising my eyebrow. "That true?"

He shifts on his feet, glaring at Levi. "Yes," he whispers harshly. "But in my defence, I feel like he's taking too much of your time. It's only fair he shares."

"Sharing is caring," Banner adds, looking like he's trying not to laugh.

I duck my head before looking up at Mark. "Did you cause bodily harm?" I ask, even though I don't see any bruises on Banner, but you never know what's hidden under the clothes.

Banner laughs, looking at Mark. "Dude, she knows you well," he tells him, not intimidated by Mark's glare, before turning back to me. "And no, he didn't touch me. But he did threaten to feed me my balls if I hurt you."

I roll my eyes, pulling my bag over my shoulder. "Well, when you're done being boys, can we go eat? I'm starving."

I look away, trying not to blush at Mark treating us like we're a couple. Call me crazy, but it's nice knowing someone can see us together. Whenever Banner and I have been in public before, I don't even get a second glance, like I'm not good enough to be with him.

"Yeah, but before we go, this got forwarded to here," Levi tells me, handing me a stack of post tied in a bow.

"My parents probably forwarded them here, I'm sure," I tell them, not looking anyone in the eye.

I let my bag fall off my shoulder and dump them inside. I'll deal with them later. I'm surprised my parents even bothered to send them. They're most likely junk mail. Or it could be their way of getting in a dig. Send the girl her mail, remind her we don't care she's gone.

When I glance up, Banner is eyeing my bag warily, so I lift it back on my shoulder and paste on a fake smile. I can tell he's come to the same conclusion as me, his jaw clenched and eyes tight.

"Right, let's go," I force out cheerfully.

∼

The pub Banner takes us to is busy. A girl's twenty-first birthday is getting rowdy, and more and more people keep turning up, even after her parents and other relatives leave.

I shift in my seat, wiping my sweaty palms on my jeans, trying not to look around.

Banner sits up straighter, and I turn to find him watching me. He grimaces, his expression filled with apology.

"I'm sorry. I've come here plenty of times with Mum and Dad when they come up, and it's never been busy. It's not big enough to be busy."

I wave him off. "It's fine. I'll deal. And I have to be in class soon."

More people file through the door, shouting their greetings to their friends, and I have to fight the urge to jump up from my seat and run out.

"No, it's not. You've gone pale as a ghost and look like you're about to vomit or pass out. I'm not sure," Banner says, sounding worried.

"He's right. Let's skip dessert and get out of here," Mark says.

"But it's my favourite part," I whine. A small group of the party head our way, banging into our chairs and making it hard for me to breathe. "Yeah, I can go without dessert."

I get up, trying to calm my breathing, and grab my bag from under the table.

"I'll get her to class and pay you guys later. That okay?" I hear Banner ask, though it sounds fuzzy.

"You go ahead, dinner is on us. Let us know when she calms down," Levi comments.

Banner takes my hand, pulling me close to him as he maneuverers us out of the bar. As soon as the doors cancel out the sound from inside, I begin to relax, lifting my face up to the cold night air.

"So much better," I gasp out.

"Did you want to catch a taxi or walk it?"

Taxi means less time with him"Walk," I tell him, not caring that it's freezing tonight.

"Can I ask you something?" he asks as he wraps his arm around my shoulders, pulling me against his chest.

"You can ask me anything."

He gulps, looking unsure, which makes me nervous. "Have you heard from your parents since you left?"

I don't really like talking about my parents. They've always been a sore subject. Even before Lara died, they treated me differently. Lara was the planned baby. And I was the surprise baby they didn't see coming, or even want, born eleven months after Lara.

From as early as I can remember, they've always reprimanded me for every little thing I did, whereas Lara could do no wrong. Lara was the wild child, always out with friends and getting into some sort of trouble. Me? I got good grades, was in by curfew, and never got into trouble. Yet, they still treated me like I was a nuisance.

"No, although I knew they wouldn't contact me before I left. I was ready for it. In a way, I'm glad. I needed a break from them. I already feel like a weight has been lifted from my shoulders. I don't feel as tense."

He scrubs a hand over his face when we stop at a set of traffic lights, waiting for the little man to turn green.

"I just don't get them. They have a great daughter, an amazing daughter, yet they treat you like this." He pauses, before inhaling. "And not to sound insensitive, but you'd think after losing one child, they'd want to be closer to the one they do have."

Even though it hurts to hear, it's nothing I haven't said to myself. "That's my parents for you. I'm used to their behaviour, but after Lara died, it got worse. She was always the buffer between us. She would somehow always be able to steer their attention away from me with stories. She would tell them what she got up to, what she got in trouble for that day, or after school clubs she joined. They wouldn't even shout at her."

"They are pretty cold people. I'm sorry to bring it up. I was just hoping they would change their minds once you were gone, but then I saw the mail. It's fucked up."

I force a laugh. "Banner, I've been competing for my parents' attention for years and never got it. I don't know why I seek their approval or want them to love me the way they love—*loved*, Lara. After she died, I stopped caring. That part inside of me that held on to hope died the day of Lara's funeral, when they wouldn't let me wear Lara's favourite dress."

We reach the university and make our way down the path that leads to the English buildings. "Sorry, but your parents are fucking wankers," he says vehemently.

I giggle, stopping in the middle of the courtyard outside the English building. "That they are."

He smiles, but I can tell it's strained. "I've got no classes tomorrow; did you want to meet up?"

Hell yes. Although we've spent time together since he got back from his away game, it's been for small amounts of time since we're both busy.

Oh crap!

"I have to meet with Jordan, the girl who showed me around, about one. You okay to meet up after?"

He grins. "A lie in for me. Score!"

I shake my head at his antics, forgetting how much he hates early mornings. "Okie doke."

We say our goodbyes before I go into the English building, heading towards Mr. Flint's class. A couple of girls sit in the hallway, reading over some papers. I walk past them, heading right into the classroom, cringing when I find I'm the only one here.

I walk to the back of the classroom, away from prying eyes and so that I'm facing the room. I can't stand people sitting behind me, it makes me feel nervous and anxious.

Unzipping my bag, I grab my books and notebook. My gaze snags on the letters and reluctantly, I pull them out. I untie the bow, flicking through my mail.

"All junk," I whisper, my eyes scanning over them. One catches my eye, and my entire body freezes.

It's from a prison.

The only person I know who's in prison is Darren.

I feel the blood drain from my face and I shove the letters back into my bag, needing to get out of here.

I can't breathe.

"Emma, you're here early. What a pleasant surprise." The deep voice startles me. I glance up, grimacing when Mr. Flint walks up the aisle towards me.

I really don't like him, but he's my teacher. No one particularly likes all their teachers. It's what I keep telling myself, anyway.

"Um, actually, I'm just leaving. I'm not feeling too good," I whisper, putting my book back in my bag.

His eyes rake over me and I fidget in my seat. He steps closer, kneeling down next to me and putting his hand on my back. He's blocking me in. Whether he's done it intentionally, I don't know, but I feel uneasy. I tense, feeling my entire body go ridged. He rubs his hand up and down my back, and bile rises in my throat.

"What's wrong? Maybe I can make you feel better," he says, but the way he said the last part sends a shiver up my spine.

I look at him, swallowing bile down and taking a deep breath. "I'd really like to go, if that's okay."

"It's your second lesson; do you really want to miss it?" he asks tightly, his hand dipping lower, nearly touching the top of my arse. I jump, a scream bubbling up my throat, but I swallow it down.

I begin to shake as I stand, causing Mr. Flint to step back, getting to his feet. He towers over me, his presence making me anxious. I move out into the aisle, shuddering when he purposely lets my body brush his, even though he could have stepped back.

"I really do have to go. If you can have someone write notes for me, I'll make sure to catch up with the work," I tell him shortly but quickly.

He grabs my arms, causing me stumble. He moves quicker than I can blink, holding onto my hips to steady me. I flinch, trying to move away, but he tightens his grip.

"Why don't you meet me here tomorrow night? I'll be happy to go over today's lesson," he says, leaning in too close for my liking.

When I move this time, he lets me go. I face him, trying my hardest to stop trembling. "I'm really sorry, but I can't. I really do have to go," I rush out, and move quickly to the door.

"I'll see you soon then, Emma," he says, amusement in his voice. I pause at the door, nodding tightly, trying to hold back tears.

I don't look back as I leave, needing out of here more than I did before. It's raining when I wobble through the exit doors. I blink up at the sky, letting the rain soak me for a few moments, just needing that feeling of peace.

When I glance around the lot, ignoring the stares of other students as they pass—most likely thinking I'm insane—I notice Banner leaning against a tree and talking on the phone.

He can't see me like this. With one look, he'll know something is wrong, and right now, I need to process what happened, then figure out what I'm going to do about the letter in my bag.

Since he hasn't noticed me, I move to the side, taking the long way around the building.

When I look back, he's still on the phone, and I pray he doesn't wait around for me to finish.

Chapter 5

After no sleep the night before, I'm wondering if it's worth cancelling with Jordan today. I just don't want to fall back into old habits; ones where I make plans and cancel them. If I cancel on her today, tomorrow it could be Banner, and after what happened in class yesterday, I need to be surrounded by people who make me feel safe. Banner is one of them.

Mark comes barging into my room just as my attention turns to the television, watching in horror as they announce a young girl has gone missing.

"Oh, my God, that's here in Whithall," I tell Mark, pointing to the TV.

He slowly sits down on the edge of the bed, his eyes never leaving the television. "Holy shit! What the fuck is happening around here? I swear this place is cursed sometimes."

I narrow my eyes at him. "You told me it was safe."

He flinches, turning to face me. "Nowhere is really safe, Em. But no one will mess with you with me around."

I sigh, my gaze still fixed on the screen as I murmur, "I know." I look away from the television, facing my cousin. "Was there something you needed?"

He faces me, too, watching me curiously. "Are you okay? You look tired."

"I was up all night, working," I lie.

He mumbles something under his breath but doesn't argue with me. "I wanted to know if you wanted a lift to Nero."

I glance at my phone, noticing it's half twelve already, and I have to meet Jordan at the coffee shop soon.

"Shit!" I look over at him, smiling. "You don't mind?"

"Nah. Me and Levi are going to check out the new fitness shop that opened up. It's just a few shops down."

"Thank you," I tell him. Then remember the letter. "Um, Mark, I got a letter yesterday" I tell him, trailing off.

He raises his eyebrow. "I know, you had a pile of them."

I shake my head at him, leaning over the bed to grab my bag. Sitting up, I pull the letter out and hand it to him.

He looks it over, his face scrunching up in confusion before it dawns on him. He glances up in horror, waving the letter in the air. "Is this from who I think it's from?"

Still shocked over it myself, I nod. "Yeah. What do you think it says?"

"Well, it can't be anything bad. They wouldn't let him send it if it was. Isn't he out soon?"

I've not wanted to think about his impending release. I avoid anything Darren related, just I like I avoid the subject of my parents. It's my way of coping.

"They called my parents a while ago to inform them he was being released in a few months. The date on the front of the letter says it was sent a month ago. Do you think my parents hid it from me?"

He eyes it again, grimacing. "Yeah, most likely. Or it got misplaced and they just found it. What I don't understand is why they allowed him to send it you. They're supposed to have a list of victims he can't write to."

"What do I do? I can't deal with that right now." I point to the letter, feeling my gut twist. "Why would he even be writing to me?"

"Do you want me to read it?"

I shake my head, and it isn't until this moment that I realise I don't want to know what it says. "No. I don't need to know. Whatever he has to say, I can't hear it."

He nods, understanding, then tears the letter in two. I watch through watery eyes, feeling a weight being lifted from my shoulders.

"All gone. Now get ready while I go put this in the shredder."

Before he can get up, I move, leaning over to wrap my arms around his shoulders. "Thank you. And thank you for letting me come here."

He hugs me back, kissing the side of my head. "I wouldn't want it any other way. Love you, cuz."

I pull back, giving him a watery smile. "Love you too."

Once he leaves, I take in a deep breath and pull myself together.

∼

Levi, Mark and I rush over to Nero, trying to avoid getting soaked in the heavy pour of rain. The sky is dark, the clouds a dark grey, promising another dreary day.

Seeing Jordan standing under shelter outside Nero, I wave and head over to her.

"Hey. I'm so sorry I'm late. We got stuck in traffic on the way here."

She smiles warmly at me. "It's fine. I've not been here long myself," she says, then looks over my shoulder. "Hey."

I glance behind me, completely forgetting Mark and Levi. "Jordan, this is my cousin, Mark, and his boyfriend, Levi."

She waves. "Nice to meet you. You joining us?"

"We've got some stuff to do, actually, but if you're here when we're finished, we'll join you. And it's good to meet you too. Thanks for showing Emma around. We were going to do it but forgot we'd booked our holiday," Mark explains.

"Sounds good. And I didn't mind. It was actually me who recommended the option to the school board. The first day I was supposed to start classes ended up with me getting lost and ending up in museums after mistaking them for a university building. Most of them look the same."

Levi laughs, nodding. "I hear ya. I took a few business courses there for part of my college course and had to ring my teacher for directions. It was embarrassing."

Mark shrugs, looking bored. "I used Google Maps."

I giggle, shaking my head at him. "Go test out the new sports drinks. I'll see you later."

"Call me if you finish before I get back."

I roll my eyes. "All right."

"See ya later," he tells us, then faces Jordan. "Nice to meet you."

"You too," Jordan tells him sincerely, smiling.

When they start off down the street, I call out to Mark, waiting for him to turn around. "Don't forget to get your Google Maps up."

His laughter echoes down to me, making me smile. He walks backwards a few steps, saluting me, before turning back around. A few girls stop and gawk and him and Levi, checking them both out and whispering to each other.

I spin around to face Jordan, taking a deep breath. "Hot chocolate?"

She moans, her eyes rolling to the back of her head, making me giggle. "Now you're talking. I've been craving one all morning, one with lots of marshmallows and chocolate powder."

I'm still giggling as we walk inside, stepping up to the counter and ordering our drinks. "I'll pay—to say thanks for showing me around."

"Thank you. I'll get the next one," she tells me, winking.

When she goes to sit down at a table near enough centre in the room, my palms begin to sweat, and my knees start to shake.

"Um, Jordan, can we, um… can we sit in the corner, maybe the one by the window?" I ask her nervously.

She looks puzzled for a second, before getting a look at my face. Her expression relaxes, and she nods. "Of course, we can."

We head over to the table, and without me saying anything, she sits in the chair that will have her back to the room, something that would have me on edge the whole time we were here.

"Thank you," I say, sighing as I take a seat.

"How are you finding it, living with your cousin?"

I beam at that. It's been great. "I love it. He and Levi are the best." I look out the window, watching the rain drip down the glass. Being with them has been the best thing that has ever happened to me. I finally feel like I can breathe. "I don't feel lonely anymore."

"You okay?" Jordan asks, snapping me out of it.

I force a smile, nodding. "Yeah. Just lost my train of thought."

"You made any friends here yet?"

"I have Banner, who I went to school with," I tell her, blushing when I think of him.

"Is he just a friend?" she teases, winking at me.

I feel my face heat, and I look away for a second. "We're just friends," I confirm.

She smiles at me knowingly. "But other than Banner?"

I shake my head. "I've not really spoken to anyone. I'm not a social person, so I don't go out much. I went to check out the library, but there was a group of boys hanging around by the door, so I went home."

"No one from class?"

Now I feel lame.

"Nope."

"I kept to myself for a few months when I started. My family live here, so I never really stuck around to make friends."

"You live close, then?"

"I do. I live about fifteen minutes away from the university. I was planning on attending Birmingham University, but my sister needed me here," she tells me, her eyes clouding.

Now it's my turn to ask if she's okay. "Are you okay?"

"Long story for another day. We're here to see how you're settling in. How are you liking Mr. Flint's class?"

As soon as she mentions his name, I feel all the blood drain from my face. My entire body is frozen to the spot and I begin to tremble all over.

I've tried not to think about Mr. Flint, but the little bit of sleep I did get, I spent having nightmares about him. I woke up still feeling his hands touching me, and his eyes watching me. My room even smelt like his cologne for a few moments. I woke up with a bad feeling, that what transpired between us in the classroom was just the beginning.

What Mr. Flint isn't prepared for is me. I won't be a push over any longer. He can't intimidate me unless I let him. And I won't. Or I'll try at least.

"Emma?" Jordan calls, and I blink back to the present.

"I'm sorry. I spaced out again. I was actually meant to ask you if there's a sign language class around here I could take."

She pauses for a second, her eyes questioning. When she doesn't ask why I avoided her question, I relax a little.

"Miss Webber, an old teacher of mine, teaches it for free at a youth centre near my house. I'm not sure if the university teach one, but if you want me to find out, I can. Or I can ask my mum to find out if Miss Webber teaches it still. They're old friends."

"I've looked online for a course at the university, but I've not found anything. If you don't mind asking your old teacher, that would be great."

"Why are you interested, if you don't mind me asking?"

"There's volunteer work going at a local play centre for children with hearing impairments. I only know some, and to volunteer, I need to know at least the basics."

"Is that the centre off of George Street?" she asks.

I nod. "You know it?"

She smiles wide. "Yeah, my mum helps run it."

"That's amazing. I've always loved volunteering. My last placement before" I drift off, realising I was about to say, 'my sister's death' to a somewhat stranger. I blink, shaking it off. "It was at a bird home. I cleaned out cages, helped feed baby parrots and some other cool stuff. I really enjoyed it."

Jordan sits forward, seeming interested. I'm used to people tuning out. It was only ever my sister or Lake who would listen to me talk about my Saturdays volunteering.

"How long have you been doing it?"

"I changed it up every six months, but I started when I was fourteen. It was hard to find places until I was sixteen. I've volunteered at a vet practice, a care home, a children's hospital, and you know about the bird home."

"It sounds amazing. I've volunteered for things, but nothing like those. It's noble of you to give so much of your time, especially so young. Most girls your age just want to go out with their friends."

I shrug, shaking my head. "I don't think it matters where you volunteer, it's the volunteering that helps. Everybody needs that little bit of extra help. And I didn't mind. I loved doing it."

"Well, I'll set up something for you, but I'm sure if you explain you'll be taking classes, they'll find something for you to do in the meantime. Can you cook or bake?"

"I can do both," I tell her, confused as to why she asked.

She beams. "Brilliant. My mum is always moaning that they don't get enough help with cooking. They do a little bake sale every few months. Maybe you'll want to help her. I help out on the day, but I can't cook for the life of me. I mess up toast," she tells me, and I begin to laugh.

"Tell her I'd love to. If you let me know how many cupcakes or cakes you want, then I can prepare what I'll need beforehand."

"I'll text her now," she says, getting her phone out.

I glance out the window, mesmerised by the rain falling onto the pavement and road. It's coming down fast now, large puddles already flooding parts of the road.

I love rain, the sound of it and being out in it. Snow and heat, I'm terrible in. I hate being cold, but I hate being hot too. I'm one of those people who complain whatever the weather.

My eyes drift over to a shop across the way, when a dark figure catches my attention. I blink, trying to get a clearer look—and notice they're staring in my direction.

The man steps forward, pulling his wet hood back, revealing his face, leaving me freezing in my seat. I blink rapidly, shaking my head.

I'm seeing things. I must be.

I turn to Jordan, who is still texting on her phone, ready to ask her if she can see the person, but when I chance a quick look back, he's gone.

I get up from my seat, causing Jordan to look up, her eyebrows lined with worry.

"You okay?" she asks, looking around the coffee shop.

No, I'm not okay.

"I have to go. I forgot I have something I need to do. Can we meet up another day?"

Her face is still creased with worry, but she nods anyway. "Do you want me to walk back with you or are you meeting your cousin?"

I grab my bag off the chair, my hands shaking. "I need Mark," I tell her, not meaning to. "I mean—I need to go to Mark."

"All right," she says softly. "Do you want me to come with you?"

"I'm fine," I tell her, zipping my coat up. "Sorry for rushing off."

"It's fine. Text me later, okay?"

I nod, waving goodbye before wobbling my way to the exit. Panic rises in my chest, and I try to breathe calmly, but it's hard when my heart is racing.

I race out the door, my head darting in every direction for any signs he's still there, that I wasn't seeing things.

"Emma," I hear called, and I jump, a scream bubbling up my throat. I hold my hand over my chest when I see Mark and Levi walking hand in hand towards me. At the sight of my cousin, a sob breaks free, tears running down my face.

I watch, frozen as he and Levi share a look before racing towards me. It doesn't take them long to reach me, and when they do, I move, falling into Mark's chest, letting him wrap me up.

Levi pulls the umbrella over us, shielding us from the rain.

"Hey, what's wrong?" Mark asks softly.

I look up, sniffling. "He's here."

He looks confused as he scans the mostly empty street. "Who?"

"Darren," I gasp out, before falling back against his chest.

Chapter 6

The second we got back, Levi steered me to my room to change into dry clothes. I opted for pyjamas, knowing I was in no fit state to leave the flat again today.

Now, I'm wrapped up in a blanket on the sofa, my knees bent to my chest. I bring my cup of tea up to my lips, wishing my hands would stop shaking. The bright side is I'm no longer having a panic attack. No, instead, I feel numb, trying to figure out if it was really Darren I saw or if my mind was playing tricks on me.

I know it was him, though. I can feel it in my bones.

I can hear Mark pacing in his room still. He's been on the phone to a bunch of people since we got back, not wanting to take chances. After I explained everything that had happened and what I saw, they were sceptic over it. I know on some level they believe me, otherwise they wouldn't be wasting their time phoning everyone, but I could see it in their eyes that they weren't sure.

Levi is sitting next to me, keeping me company, worried I'll have another panic attack.

I don't know what I'd do if I didn't have these two in my life. Mark was there as much as he could be when there was distance between us and has done more for me than I ever could have imagined since I moved here. It feels foreign to have someone care for me so deeply.

If I had told my parents what happened today, they would have told me to grow up and stop acting like a snivelling child. They wouldn't have worried over me, or cared that it was Darren, the lad who had a hand in killing their daughter. Somehow, it's me they blame for her death, not him. There's no reasoning.

Someone bangs on our door, making me jump from my seat. I look over my shoulder at the door, my eyes round as fear shoots up my spine.

What if it's him?

I feel sick.

I jump, looking back over at Levi when he places his hand on my knee. "It's okay, it's only Banner. I'll get it."

I nod, trying to calm my racing heart, but I'm still not fully with it. I feel him get up and hear the door open but keep my eyes on my cup of tea.

Banner is next to me within a second. I glance up, feeling my eyes water. I refuse to cry any more though. I've cried enough.

"He won't touch you again, I swear. And if I have anything to do with it, he won't get near you again, either," he grits out. I open my mouth to argue that he can't be with me for every second of the day, but he shocks me when he lifts me up. He manages to do it with me still wrapped up in my blanket, my cup of tea in hand. He turns, gently sitting down in the seat I was sitting in, keeping me in his arms on his lap.

"I can sit over there, you know," I tell him, pointing the end of the sofa, not sure what to do with our closeness.

He shakes his head, and he looks like he's struggling to reign in his temper "No, I just need to hold you. When Mark called me, I kept thinking the worst. What happened? I kind of ended the call and raced over here."

"I was at the café with Jordan. I was looking out the window and I saw him. At first, I wasn't sure who it was as they had their hood up, but then he pulled it down and I saw him. I looked away for a split second, then he was gone."

"And you've not seen him before today?" he asks.

I shake my head. "No."

Banner nods, running his finger down my cheek before turning to Levi, who has taken up residence on the two-seater sofa. "Have you heard anything?"

Levi looks behind us to where Mark is pacing in his room on the phone. "We're just waiting to see what the solicitor says. Emma should have been given notice of his release date."

"It's a fucking joke. They should have given him a restraining order," Banner bites out, squeezing me against him.

I sigh, dropping my head against the crook of his neck, my gaze fixed on Levi.

"I don't know what they did or didn't do. We're still not sure if it was him she saw or not."

Banner tenses, his head moving to look down at me. "What do you mean, you aren't sure."

I pull back a little, so I can see him. "It was raining. But I'm ninety-five percent sure it was him. It was like I said: one minute he was there, the next he wasn't," I tell him quietly. I bite my bottom lip, wondering if I should tell him about the letter. The one Mark destroyed this morning before we left to meet Jordan.

"We're waiting to see what they say before we jump to conclusions," Levi says, looking away. They believed me when I said I saw someone, they just don't know yet if it was Darren.

"If she said she saw him, then she saw him. She has no reason to lie or to conjure him up."

I place my hand on his chest, not wanting him to get riled up. "I do, actually."

He looks more confused than he did before. "What do you mean? What aren't you telling me?"

My eyes flicker to Levi, and not missing a beat, he gets up from his seat. "I'll give you two some privacy and see what Mark has found out."

He leaves us alone and Banner shifts me, so I can look up at him better. "Talk?"

I take a deep breath and start from the beginning. "Remember the stack of letters I got yesterday?" He nods, so I continue. "I went through them in class last night, since I was early. I found a letter from the prison. From Darren."

I gasp when he lifts me off him, dropping me gently on the seat next to us. The hurt on his face instantly makes me feel guilty. He runs his fingers through his hair, looking at me like I just told him someone died. I hate that I've hurt him by not telling him straight away. I don't want to see him look at me like this again, it's breaking my heart.

"Why didn't you tell me? What did it say?" he asks.

I place my hand on his bouncing knee. "I didn't want to worry you, and honestly, I wanted to pretend it wasn't there. I'm still shocked I received one from him. I don't know what he would have to say, and frankly, I don't want to know."

"You didn't read it?" he asks, his eyes round.

I shake my head. "No. I didn't want to deal with it."

"Where is it now? If he's contacting you and now following you, we need to go to the police with it. Maybe they can issue a restraining order or something."

He's so goddamn caring, it's humbling. But it's not as easy as us going to the police. They'll be questions, so many damn questions; one's I don't want to answer. It will bring back too many memories for me.

The court case for Darren nearly broke me. I've been in scary situations—I found my sister dead, for Christ sakes—but being in that court room made me feel dirty, like I was the criminal and not the victim. I felt judged, and not in a good way.

I have to look away when those memories surface. I feel dirty all over again. "Mark destroyed it this morning for me. I couldn't touch it for a second longer—or look at it. That part of my life was horrible, Banner. I didn't want to be reminded of it all over again. I'm doing better than I was twelve months ago. Whatever was in that letter, nothing good could come out of it. Whether he's written something good or something bad, it won't make me feel any better."

He pulls me against him, hugging me tight as he kisses the top of my head. "Fuck, I'm an idiot. I didn't think of it like that. I'm fucking sorry, Em." He pauses, pulling back, his eyes fierce and jaw set. "I'm just worried about you. I know how hard you've worked to get where you are today. I don't want you to go back to that dark place. It killed me seeing you like that. If that dickhead is back, I don't want him setting your recovery back."

I never knew he felt like that. It makes me feel warm inside that he cares that much. Banner may have known about me before my sister and the incident with Darren, but he's only ever known who I am now. He's never asked when I'll be back to my old self again, not like my other friends did. In the end, they got fed up with trying and left. I was fine with that. But Banner… he's always been there, and he likes who I am now, not who I was.

So, when he says something so incredibly sweet and caring, I know it's meaningful, and that he truly believes what he's saying.

"I will admit, it's shocked and scared me that he's here. *He* scares me. I still have nightmares. Not as regularly as I used to, but they are there, always ready to spring up on me." I pause, taking a deep breath. "Earlier could have been my mind playing tricks on me. I'd gotten that letter and, consciously, it was still on my mind. When I looked out that window It was him, Banner. I know it was. I could feel it," I tell him adamantly.

"I believe you. I've known you a long time, and I know you wouldn't worry people on a guess. Did you book to see a new therapist? If he's back, talking to a professional about it will help."

I nod. I hate talking about this part of my life to him. It makes me look weak, and I don't want him to see me like that. I want him to see me as the strong woman I know I can be. Not someone he pities.

"I do. Her name's Milly Everhert. She deals with rape and abuse victims, so I wasn't sure she'd take my case, but I heard she was the best and doesn't hold her sessions in some stuffy office. I'll be meeting her next Friday, before class."

Something dawns across his expression. "I think I know who you're talking about. She funds the counselling that is happening at the university for the victims involved in the rape case last year."

"She does?" I ask.

"Yeah. She's meant to be really good. I only know about her because a friend of mine on the rugby teams' sister attends the meetings they set up."

Our conversation comes to an end when Mark and Levi walk back into the room, their expressions grim.

That can't be good—whatever they have to say.

"What?" I ask, already dreading their answer.

They sit down in the two-seater, eyeing me warily. "Are you sure you want to know this?" Mark asks, and I know it's because he's remembering back to last year, and how withdrawn I had got.

"I need to know. I'll go crazy otherwise. What did they say?"

He shares a look with Levi before facing me. "First, I've spoken to your parents."

I stare for a few moments, my mouth agape, before snapping out of it. "What? Why?" I ask, angry he would betray me like that. He has no right, and I tell him so. "You had no right to speak to them, Mark. Why would you call them when you know they don't care about me?"

"She's right. What the fuck, mate. You're meant to be family," Banner bites out.

Levi holds his hand up, always the mediator. "Listen to what he has to say before jumping the gun. He didn't ring to update them on you or what happened, I promise."

I nod, looking at Mark and silently telling him to get on with it.

"I called the lawyer you said you used first, just to see what they had to say. They told me they sent a letter out to your parents' address a few months ago—three to be exact—with the details of Darren's release date. The letter was addressed to you as you're no longer a minor. His release date has long passed, Emma. It was him."

I gasp at hearing he was here, and that my parents hid that letter from me—if it was even sent. I can't see them being that malicious. "So, it was him?" I ask, wanting them to confirm I'm not going mad. "I can't see Mum and Dad hiding a letter from me. It could have been anything. Maybe it got lost in the post."

He winces, opening his mouth, then closing it, looking torn. Levi takes his hand, and I watch as he rubs his thumb over the top, soothingly. I look away, feeling a knot in my throat. They should just spit it out. The suspense is killing me. I already know what they're going to say; I can feel it.

"It was Darren, but I'll get back to that in a second. I just need to tell you that your parents knew," he bites out, gritting his teeth. "They admitted it on the phone when I asked, when I threatened to call our grandparents if they didn't tell me the truth. They said you didn't deserve to know, that you would only cause them more stress."

He looks away, his chest rising and falling as his jaw clenches.

Those words shouldn't hurt, but they do. I know my parents don't love me, but it still feels like someone is squeezing my heart and twisting it every time they pull something else.

"They knew he was being released?" I whisper, letting Banner hug me closer.

He nods sadly. "They did. I've informed the lawyer you weren't notified."

"And what did they say about Darren?" Banner asks.

"He got released just under a month ago. He never moved back home with his parents, but with his aunt, not far from here."

"Here?" I squeal, my body shaking again. I don't know how I feel about the notion of bumping into him all the time. I thought moving away from home before he got released would ease my anxiety, but now he's here, where I'm trying to make a fresh start.

"Yeah. They're going to check in with his probation officer, but according to the lawyer, a restraining order wasn't issued before his release because your mum and dad never requested one."

"You've got to be fucking kidding me?" Banner growls.

I look down at my lap, holding back tears. "So, he's free to come near me?" I ask hoarsely.

"We won't let him. I've asked the lawyer to find out if there's anything we can do and explained the earlier incident. They weren't even aware of your change of address, so he's not broken any laws. But that's not saying he won't. I can promise we won't let him touch you."

"I can't believe this is happening. This is meant to be my fresh start. What if he decides to get payback because I sent him to prison?"

"For a crime he committed," Banner reminds me softly.

"He didn't care that it was his fault my sister died. What makes you think he'll care that he got sent to prison for something that was his fault?"

Banner starts running his hand up and down my arm. "Do not take this the wrong way, because I hate the fucker just as much as you, but back then, he was irrational. He was on too many drugs and wasn't thinking clearly. I know it doesn't excuse what he did to you, but I think—well, *hope*—he's owning up to his mistakes."

I tried telling myself he attacked me because of the drugs, but deep down inside, Darren has a dark side. Can he redeem himself? I'm not sure. I'd like to hope I'm the kind of person that would think so, that somewhere inside of me, I can find forgiveness. But after everything he did to me, took from me… it's all too fresh. He'd have to do something seriously redeemable to prove to me he's changed, and that in a few months, when his probation period is over, he won't turn back to drugs—if he hasn't already.

I shake my thoughts away, not wanting to think about this anymore. It will just play on my mind until I finally manage to sleep, conjuring up different future scenarios.

"Can we talk about something else? I can't deal with any more and talking about it won't help. It will just keep going around in my head until I find a solution that will deal with it. At the moment, that's impossible, because I'm going to avoid him at all costs."

"Of course," Levi says.

"Anything."

"My roommate got hammered and shit the bed after eating some bad Chinese food," Banner blurts out, falling back against the sofa.

We all turn in his direction, pausing for a moment before bursting into laughter.

"Well, that wasn't random and awkward at all," Levi tells us, chuckling.

"I can't be arsed to cook. Does anyone want a particular takeaway?" Mark asks.

"Not Chinese," Banner and I say, not after hearing about his roommate.

We glance at each other before laughing.

"Pizza it is," Levi laughs, getting up to grab his phone.

"I'll go grab some drinks. Banner, do you want a beer?" Mark asks.

"Yeah, go on then," Banner replies.

Once he's out of the room, Banner shifts so he's facing me. "I know you want to forget everything for a bit, but I need to know if you're really doing okay. That was a lot to digest," he says, his forehead creased.

"I'm not sure. I have you guys, though, so I know I'll be fine in the end."

"No, you'd be fine whether you had us or not. You're the strongest person I know," he tells me, shocking me speechless. "Whatever happens though, I'll be here. I'll always be here."

It's moments like this that I question his feelings towards me. One moment he acts like he's a friend, then the next, he'll say something so incredibly sweet, and it makes me wonder if he has feelings for me too; more than just being my friend.

My feelings run deeper, and not because he was there for me at the worst time of my life. I fell for his touches, his smiles, hearing him laugh and talk. I fell for the person he is and for the person he makes me believe I can be when I'm around him. He makes me feel special, like a mythical creature.

I glance up from my lap, swallowing past the knot in my throat. "I know you'll be there. I'm lucky to have you."

He expression relaxes, his gaze never wavering from mine. "I'm the lucky one."

Something passes between us, shifting in the air, neither of us looking away. He moves—I move. But before anything can happen, Levi and Mark walk back in and the pull between us breaks.

"Food's on its way," Levi says, sitting down.

"Here you go," Mark says to Banner, handing him a beer.

Banner clears his throat, taking the beer. "Thanks," he tells him hoarsely.

Mark turns to me. "I got you a Vimto."

I smile, taking the can from him. "Thanks, Mark."

"What movie do you fancy watching?" he asks, walking over to the row of DVD's.

I can't look at Banner, but I can feel his stare on the side of my face. "I don't mind. Just nothing too gory."

"Banner?" Mark calls, looking at him for ideas.

"Um, I don't mind. I'm easy."

For the first time since our friendship began, I feel uneasy. My body is stiff, unsure whether I should move over to the other side of the sofa. My unspoken question is answered when Banner pulls me against him, shifting so his feet are up on the sofa and I'm lying against his chest. He pulls the blanket over us, and I sigh, feeling warm.

It takes a few moments to relax, but when I do, Banner starts running his fingers through my hair.

It's not long into the movie when my eyes begin to drift shut and I fall into a restful sleep.

Chapter 7

I'm lost in the story I'm working on when I hear movement coming from inside my bedroom. Banner has been staying the past few days. He said it's because he's too lazy to go home, but I know it's because he's worried about me.

The first couple of days, he slept on the sofa out here, but the last two, he's fallen asleep in bed with me whilst watching a movie. It's been nice—being intimately close to him and spending more than an hour or two at a time together. I sound like a stalker, but I grew up without feeling any warmth or love from my parents. My sister loved me, and we were close, but she loved everyone. She was a wild child, went where the mood took her. With Banner... we click. I feel warm and loved when he's around, and for me, that's everything. It's why I'm so scared to show him just how much he means to me. I can't lose him.

When the door to my room opens, I snap my laptop shut, knowing Banner will fight to read it.

I look over the back of the sofa, smiling when he walks out in just his tracksuit bottoms and no shirt, rubbing sleep from his eyes.

"Morning," I call out.

He groans, walking around the sofa and dropping himself next to me. "I can't believe I'm still tired and it's nearly noon," he says groggily. "Why didn't you wake me up?"

"Because you've been getting up at five every morning to go to practice, and then going to classes. You said last night you had the morning and most of the afternoon free, so I turned your alarm off this morning when I got up." I shrug, like it's no big deal, blushing when his expression softens.

He keeps staring at me like I just spent millions on him. I only turned his alarm off to let him get some rest.

"You know, you really are amazing."

My cheeks heat further, and I try to play it off. "I am, aren't I?"

He chuckles as he shuffles closer, his arm touching mine. "So, you excited to meet Lake and her boyfriend tomorrow?"

A smile spreads across my face. "I am. We talk all the time through email and text, sometimes over the phone, but I miss her. She's really happy, the happiest I've ever seen her."

"She's got her family back and a new family added to it," he says softly.

My smile falls a little, wishing I had that, and hoping I find that here with Mark, Levi and Banner. "Yeah. They were a small family, but now she has a huge one. They seem really nice—a little crazy, but she fits in," I tell him. "I hear them over the phone, teasing her or someone else in the background. It's funny."

"What time are we meeting her?"

"She texted me saying her boyfriend's brother is going to drop them off, then he's going to the zoo with his kids or something. I'm not sure. They're going to meet us here, then we're going to head to that café Jordan told me about. The one near the university."

He thinks about it for a minute. "Fun 'N Cups?"

I giggle at the name. "Yeah, that one. Have you been there before?"

"Yeah, I go for lunch most days. They do the best burgers in town. They're huge."

"I honestly don't know where you put it," I tell him, eyeing his hard stomach, his muscles. I look away, feeling my cheeks heat.

"I'm just fucking awesome," he says, making me laugh. "Oh, before I forget, I have to go to a meeting the coach has scheduled before class, so I won't be able to spend the rest of the day with you. You've got a class tonight, don't you?"

"I do. Mr. Flint wanted us to come in, so he can set our coursework for the term. It should only take an hour at the most. He didn't want it to take up our lesson time tomorrow as we already only have small amounts of time each night."

"What time do you have to be there? My classes finish at five today, but then I have to go meet Tom, who is working with me for a class we have to prepare for."

"What do you mean?"

"We've been assigned different subjects to teach, which we'll demonstrate in front of our class first, then onto another school. The teacher will grade us based on our technique, approach etc."

That sounds awesome, and pretty scary. He wants to teach teenagers once he's finished earning his degree. Why he would want to do that, I don't know. It wasn't long ago he was playing up in the classroom at high school.

"What's the subject you're teaching?" I ask, knowing he wants to teach biology.

His cheeks turn bright pink, and he doesn't look at me when he answers. "STD's."

My mouth gapes open for a moment before I burst out laughing. When I sober, I clutch my stomach from the ache and face him, trying hard not to start laughing again.

"Just one, or all of them?"

He groans, his head dropping back against the top of the sofa. "Just the common ones, then how to treat and cure them. In our written presentation we have to talk about the cells and how it's caused etc."

"Will there be diagrams?" I ask, raising an eyebrow. I bite my lip to stop myself from laughing when he rolls his head to the side, narrowing his eyes at me.

"You think this is funny?"

I press my lips together, shaking my head. The second he sits up, looking like someone ran over his puppy, I burst out laughing.

When he brings his hands up, coming towards me, I squeal, knowing what's coming. I can see it in his eyes, and the little smirk he has playing on his lips.

"No, no, no," I wail, falling back on the sofa.

I'm laughing so hard, I can barely see him through my watery eyes when he settles above me. Just as I start to wriggle free, his hands come down, his fingers digging in to my sides as he tickles me.

"Stop!" I cry out, feeling my bladder about to burst.

"Nope, not until you promise to stop teasing me."

I shake my head. "Nope. Never!"

"Then I won't stop," he says, settling between my legs. He brings his face down, and before I can pull away, he's blowing raspberries in the crook of my neck.

My sides hurt from laughing, and I'm close to peeing my pants, but it doesn't stop me from answering him back. "Will it be at an all-girl school?"

"You little"

"Genius?"

He chuckles, so close I can feel his breath on my face. He stops twisting and digging his fingers into my sides as his face loses all expression. We're both breathing hard, gazing into each other's eyes. I lick my lips, and he tracks the movement. I hear him groan, his eyes closing for a moment, like he's restraining himself.

My breath comes out in soft gasp when I feel something hard pressing against my leg. I start breathing heavily for other reasons as a throbbing sensation starts between my legs.

Without thinking, I raise my hand to cup his cheek. His lips part, his eyes dilating. He starts to lower his head, but a key being put into the lock of the front door startles us. I end up pushing him off me. I gasp, wanting the ground to swallow me up. I'm so embarrassed.

I sit up quickly, looking down at Banner groaning on the floor, and wince. "I'm so sorry," I whisper-yell.

His eyes open, and he winks, but I can see the grimace when he tries to sit up. "It's fine."

He manages to stand as the door opens, and Levi walks in, looking troubled. When he looks up, his eyes widen in surprise. "Banner, I thought you'd be gone by now."

Banner looks at the clock hanging above the fireplace. "Nah, I got another twenty minutes. Why, were you missing me?"

"No. But I was just about to ask Emma to call you. Any chance you don't have any tattoos on the back of your leg?" Levi asks, looking hopeful.

Banner doesn't seem fazed by the question. "My right is bare. Why?"

"Any chance you would let me tattoo a piece of art onto you? My volunteer broke both of his legs and won't be out of his casts for another eight weeks."

"He broke both of his legs?" I ask, wondering if Levi just got told a load of bull. Who breaks both of their legs?

Levi closes his eyes for a second, groaning in frustration. "Yes. The fucker was doing one of his YouTube videos. He jumped from the roof of his house onto a trampoline."

"A trampoline," Banner and I say simultaneously.

"Yeah. The trampoline broke and he landed on both feet. Broke his right one in three places and his left in two. He's lucky the bone didn't snap through skin, or that he didn't damage his spine."

Banner and I look at each other before facing Levi. "What's his YouTube account name?" Banner asks, beating me to it.

Levi looks between us, then rolls his eyes. "You can't watch that shit?"

"We do," we say, chuckling at his expression.

"Can you do it? It's for a competition in a magazine I entered, and the piece can take a few sessions."

Banner nods. "If the art is good, then yeah."

"Thank you. I'll bring it home later. You staying again?"

Banner glances my way, silently questioning me. I shrug. "If you want to. I don't mind."

Levi relaxes when he nods to say he's staying. "How come you're back early?" I ask.

"I came to ask if you'd ring Banner. I was panicking. I've waited ages to get this spot in the magazine."

"Why didn't you ask me?"

Levi and Banner share a look, before Levi addresses me. "It's a big tattoo."

"And?"

"And it's painful. It's not something you'd have for a first tattoo. And it's drawn for a male."

I roll my eyes. "It can't hurt that bad. Are you saying I couldn't handle it?"

Levi steps back, looking to Banner for help. When Banner takes his own step back, his hands in the air, I roll my eyes.

"I didn't say you couldn't handle it. I just wouldn't recommend something that big for your first time. Once you've had one and you know you can tolerate the pain, then look into getting a bigger one."

"Good. Let's go, then," I tell him, walking over to the chair next to the front door and picking up my bag.

Levi and Banner are still standing in the same position when I turn around, watching me like I've lost my mind.

Banner snaps out of it first. "You can't have your first tattoo without me there."

I smile at that, remembering the time he was telling me he was going to take me when I was better. He didn't know it then, but I was looking forward to it.

"You've got a meeting to go to, remember," I remind him.

He shrugs, rolling his eyes as he pulls his phone out. "I'll text Rafner to let them know I'll be running late. He'll be there early. I wouldn't miss this for the fucking world."

"Let's go, then," I tell them, giving Levi an imploring look.

He shakes out of his shock, and nods. "Okay, then. But if Mark asks, you totally begged me."

I giggle. Mark doesn't have a say; he's covered in tattoos, just like Levi and Banner.

As we leave, the bounce in my step is evident.

I'm getting a tattoo, something I never thought I'd do, since I've always been afraid of needles. I can't think of the pain all three have mentioned when we've spoken about theirs, otherwise I'll chicken out.

And this is a tattoo I really want.

~

I'm impressed with the shop Levi has set up. He has six different rooms in one space, the tops of the doors fitted with glass, but the bottom made of solid, dark wood to give each client privacy. The counter at the front is painted black, and the front of the shop it is covered in pictures and photographs of tattoos they've done. It's great, and not at all how I pictured a tattoo studio. I imagined loads of skulls, snakes, and rock and roll on the walls, but instead, there is art. Beautiful, incredible art.

"Levi, this place is amazing," I tell him, before my focus snags on a woman getting her thigh tattooed, the door to the room she's in slightly ajar. She doesn't even flinch when he scrapes the needle across her skin.

Banner nudges me, and I look away, embarrassed I was caught staring when the woman only has on a small pair of shorts.

"Sorry, did I miss something?" I ask.

They both laugh at me, and my cheeks heat.

"Follow me," Levi says through his deep chuckles.

I follow him to a room at the back where a black chair that looks like it belongs in a dental clinic sits. On the side are bottles of lotions, a pile of tissues, cling film, and other bits and bobs. The machine next to the chair catches my eye for a few seconds before I start looking at the row of little bottles of ink on the shelf under the window.

"This is all amazing. If I had any artistic abilities, I'd totally be doing this. How long have you been doing it again?"

He chuckles as he sits down in his seat, gesturing for me to sit down in the dentist chair. I know it's not, but that's what I'm going to call it.

"I started doing it when Dad bought me my first gun at sixteen. I've been doing it, qualified, for six years, though. I love doing it."

"I can see why. Some of these are fucking sick," Banner says, flicking through a folder.

I try to peer over at the images but he's too far away to see.

"Cheers," Levi tells him, before turning to me, smiling. "Right, what do you want? A butterfly, star, dolphin?"

I roll my eyes at him, then turn to Banner. "He has it."

Banner, hearing, looks up. "I have it?"

I chuckle at his puzzled expression. I'm a little nervous. I have no idea how he's going to take it when I tell him what tattoo I want. "Yes. He has a semicolon on his thumb. I want it on the inside of my wrist," I tell him, then swallow nervously. "And can you put Lara's name in the middle, in script, please?"

Levi turns serious, clearing his throat. "I can do that."

I try not to look at Banner whilst Levi starts setting stuff up. But when he wheels his chair over to me, I have to. He's a hard person to ignore.

"You really want it?"

"Yeah. Do you think she'd like it?" I ask him, feeling a knot in my throat. He runs a finger down my cheek, and I soak in his warmth, closing my eyes briefly.

When I open them, the fierceness in his gaze has me catching my breath. "I think she'd love it. And she'd be fucking proud you're going through with this."

I laugh at that. "If she were here, she'd be teasing me, telling me not to cry."

His smile is blinding. "Well, I have two shoulders, so if you want to cry, cry away. If you want to squeeze my hand, go ahead. But don't break my fingers; I need them. If you need to bite something, you're on your own," he tells me, and I burst out laughing.

"You ready?" Levi asks, and I turn my attention to him.

My forehead creases when he raises the disposal razor. "Um, Levi, you do know I came for a tattoo, not beauty treatment, don't you?"

Both he and Banner laugh. "It's to shave the area," Banner says, whilst Levi composes himself.

I blush, feeling stupid. "Oh."

"Ready?"

I nod, watching as he wipes the area, shaves, then wipes it again. "Don't you need a stencil or something?"

"I can freehand. Once I'm done, you check it to see if it's perfect, then I'll tattoo it."

I nod, relaxing back into the chair whilst he draws on my wrist. The feel of the pen on my skin is relaxing, almost making me sleepy.

I roll my head to face Banner. "Can you see if it's in a good place? I want to see it for the first time when it's done."

He nods, looking over to Levi, who has stopped drawing. "That's perfect."

I hold my breath when I hear the tattoo gun start buzzing, my heart beating rapidly against my chest.

As soon as the needle pierces my skin, I go lightheaded, more from the adrenaline running through my system, as so far, the pain is bearable.

I keep my gaze locked on Banner's, but from the corner of my eye, I notice his phone pointed in Levi's direction.

"Are you recording me?" I ask, my voice tight when my skin starts to sting and burn in one particular spot.

"Yes. You'll want to see this later." He grins, taking my hand in his. I squeeze his hand, grateful for him being here, especially when he's missing a meeting with his coach.

The buzzing stops and continues, the burning so bad in places that I have to grit my teeth and close my eyes.

It will be worth it though. I know it.

"How you feeling?" Levi asks, and Banner's eyes come to me, waiting for my answer.

"Good. It stings a little more in certain places, but other than that, it's fine. It just feels like tiny cat scratches."

He chuckles. "Some places are more tender on the wrist. Let me know if you need a minute, okay?"

I nod, but then realise he's probably looking down at what he's doing—well, I hope he is. "I will. I promise."

"Have you got a sleeping bag?" Banner asks randomly.

I shake my head. I've only ever been camping a few times. "No. Why?"

"I have a tent for us to share, but I'll have to get a list of what else you'll need. I'll grab you it when I go to get a new sleeping bag. Todd was smoking a spliff and burnt holes in my last one."

"You smoke weed?" I ask, shocked.

He scoffs. "No. I'll never touch the stuff. I want my brain cells intact, thank you."

I relax a little, not knowing how I would feel if he had answered differently. Drugs have affected my life so badly, and I've never touched anything other than prescription tablets.

"That's good—not about your sleeping bag, but that you don't do drugs."

His eyes shine with laughter when he smirks at me. "I don't need drugs to have a good time or relax. I'm too mellow for that shit."

I giggle at that. "You are the light of the party."

He grins, looking sexy as ever. "There isn't a party until I'm there."

A thought occurs to me. "So, you've never done drugs?"

He pauses, thinking about it. "I think I tried weed at the back of the school field once, but once was enough for me to cough up a lung and swear to never do that shit again."

I laugh at that. "So, you were completely sober when you climbed out of Mrs. Waldwick's classroom window and down the drain pipe?"

He looks away for a second, his cheeks turning pink. I smile wider. "Sober as a judge. I saw a group of friends heading out of school, so I joined them. Didn't want the teacher stopping me out in the hall and asking where I was going."

I shake my head, laughing. "Or when you ran around the dinner hall butt naked with only a football covering your... your, um... your junk?" I ask, feeling my cheeks heat.

He chokes on his laughter. "Unfortunately, no. I wish I had been. It was Miss Drum that caught me. I lost a bet with the lads."

I giggle, wishing I could have seen Miss Drum's reaction. She was such a hard-arse teacher. If you sneezed, she gave you detention. She was so strict, everybody hated taking history with her.

"What did she do?"

He ducks his head when he answers. "Dragged me by my ear to the principal's office. She pulled so hard I dropped the ball."

I burst out laughing, seriously wishing I could have seen that. I bet she lost her shit.

"All done," Levi says, shocking me.

"Already?" I ask, turning to face him.

"He did good distracting you." Levi winks, putting his stuff away.

I look down at my wrist, feeling my eyes water. In a beautiful script, Lara's name is written in the middle of the semicolon.

A tear falls as I look up at Levi, feeling my throat tighten. "I love it. Thank you so much."

He looks away, his own eyes going misty. "Anything for you."

I nod, looking down at my wrist before turning to bring it closer to Banner, showing him. "Isn't it beautiful?"

"Yeah," he says, sounding choked up. I look up, my heart stopping when I find him staring at me and not my tattoo.

"I've got some cream at home for you to put on, so all you have to do when you get back is lightly run a wet cloth over it. I'll put the cream on tonight before you go to bed."

"Thank you again, Levi. I couldn't have pictured anything better. It's perfect."

Banner gets up, leaning over and kissing my forehead. "I'm proud of you. You did it."

I look up, giving him a watery smile. "You thought I'd chicken out?"

He chuckles quietly. "No. Like I've told you a million times: you're the strongest and bravest person I know. I just meant you got your first tattoo."

"Just wait until the next time something inspires me," I tell him as I get up, looking over my shoulder to wink at him.

"Come on. I'll drop you at home and then get to this meeting."

"I can't wait to show Lake. She hates needles too."

"Maybe she'll get one next," Banner says, handing me my bag.

We turn to Levi, who is just cleaning down his workspace. "What do I owe you?"

Levi looks up, smiling. "Nothing. You'll never have to pay for a tattoo with me."

"Are you sure?" I ask, biting my bottom lip.

"Yep, now get going before you make lover-boy late."

Banner scoffs—used to Levi and Mark's nickname for him. "See ya later, mate."

I wave goodbye, heading out of the shop, tucked under Banner's arm. I can't stop staring at my wrist, proud of myself for going through with it. It's something I'm going to treasure forever, never regretting having it because the tattoo means more to me than people will know.

Chapter 8

I hug my arms around myself tighter, whilst trying to keep a hold of the umbrella. It's pouring down with rain, the wind picking up and sending a chill through me, even though I'm wrapped up in a winter coat, a hat, scarf and gloves.

What I'd wish to be at home, curled up on the sofa watching a sappy love story on the television. But no, Mr. Flint called us in on a day we don't normally attend so he could go over our coursework for the term.

Mr. Flint is late, and for some reason, the front entrance to the English building is locked. I have no idea what is going on or what the protocol is when a teacher doesn't turn up. At high school, if a teacher was ten minutes late, we could go to the dinner hall until the next class.

I glance around the sea of faces waiting to be let inside to see if one of them can help me. They all seem to be talking in groups, or with a friend. There is no way I have the courage to walk up to one and interrupt what they are doing. I'd make a fool out of myself, or most likely get ignored when I call 'excuse me' to get their attention.

When I see a girl standing under the tree, even though thunder and lightning is on the horizon, I decide to approach her. Unlike the others, she's alone—like me. As I approach her, the other students begin walking off. I look around, puzzled, wondering if I missed something or if they're going home, sick of standing in the rain.

Not wanting to stay standing in the dark on my own, I pick up my steps. She's reading something on her phone when I reach her.

"Hey, do you know what's going on? Where is everyone going?"

"Did you not get the text?" she asks bluntly, glancing up from her phone.

I shake my head, not realising the university sent out texts. I check my phone just in case, and other than a text from Banner saying he's heading back to mine, I don't have a message.

"No. What did it say?"

"It just said the front entrance was under maintenance and to use the side door," she tells me, pulling her hood back over her head when the wind blows it off.

I lift the umbrella over her, so she's covered, and she smiles gratefully. "Do you know where it is? I have no idea. This is the only entrance I was told about."

"Yeah. I took a different class last year that was through that entrance. Come on, we can walk together."

"Thank you," I tell her, breathing a sigh of relief. "I'm Emma, by the way."

"Becky."

"You took night courses last year?" I ask, starting conversation. I feel awkward with the silence. I'm also curious as this was the first late-night English class they've done. The others are usually done through term breaks.

I feel her gaze on the side of my face, but I keep looking at my feet, watching where I'm going before I trip and fall. Also, eye contact with strangers makes me nervous.

"I get bored. I've got a job at an accounting agency, so this is my only time to do it."

"You get bored?" I ask dubiously. Why on earth would she take classes when she's bored, instead of taking up a hobby? And if she already has a job in accountancy, why start up another course?

Bizarre.

She laughs at my expression. "I know, I know. I get that look all the time. I love learning, though. I took an accountancy course first, then an electrical engineering course, and have even got qualifications for piercings, childminding, and a few other things. I'm also a qualified phlebotomist."

I gape at her in shock. *She really is bored.* "What the hell is a phlebotomist?" I ask, hoping I said it correctly.

She giggles as we reach the side door. "I take people's blood. I still do it on Saturdays at the local blood bank. I enjoy it, but there's no way I could do it to earn a living."

I look at her in wonder as I put my umbrella down, shaking off the rain before stepping inside the building. I'm just through the door when a cold shiver runs down my spine. The feeling of someone watching me has my heart beating wildly against my chest. I scan the area outside, but with the dark shadows and pouring rain, it's hard to see past what's in front of me.

"Are you okay?" Becky asks, stepping forward so we're side by side in the doorway.

I paste on a fake smile. "Yeah." I shake my head, clearing my throat. "I can't believe you do so much. It's incredible. Why are you taking English? You don't have to answer—I'm just really curious."

I'd love to know, too. There is so much you can do with an English degree. I'd like to know what she plans to use it for.

"Something to do, really," she says, shrugging. "And it never hurts to improve on certain subjects."

I laugh, in awe of the girl standing in front of me. "And accountancy; why did you choose that?"

"I excel at it. I've always been good with numbers."

When we reach our classroom, I stop just outside the door, facing her. "Before we go in, I have to know; why an electrical engineering course?"

This one has me interested the most. You don't meet many girls who can claim they are an electrician. I'm not being sexiest; it's just a fact. I don't know one, but then again, I don't know any male ones, either.

Also, an electrician… It's so random, it's not even funny. There must be a story behind it.

Her amused gaze turns to me. "I own my own house and I kept having trouble with the electrics. The companies I kept calling would send men round who thought they could take advantage of a girl living alone and charge me twice as much as what the work costs. Now I can sort my own damn electrics out. I tried to do plumbing when the drain in my back garden got blocked, but the second I had the water company out and smelled the stench, I cancelled my application."

I giggle, finding her intriguing. "I wouldn't want to, either, after smelling something like that." We step inside, and my shoulders relax when I don't find Mr. Flint leaning back against his desk. I turn to Becky, hoping we can be friends and meet up sometime in the future. "Enjoy the class."

"You too."

I go to walk off, when she calls me. I turn to face her. "Yeah?"

"Here, take my number," she tells me, handing me a card. "It's hard to make friends when I'm socially awkward, but you seem like a cool person."

I bite back a smile at her words. "Thanks. If you ever want to grab a cup of coffee, let me know. I'll text you my number now."

She nods and takes a seat at the front of the class without another word. I make my way to the back, ignoring the lads' eyes on me when I pass them. I'm getting used to it now. There aren't many in here, but the ones that are look like they don't want to be. That either means they're failing their class and need to take the extra lessons or have to for something else. None look willing.

I type out a quick text to Becky before I forget to send her my number.

ME: This is my number.

BECKY: Who is this?

My eyes scrunch together at her reply. When I look up to make sure she didn't give me the wrong number, I notice her staring at her phone with the same confusion. I bite back laughter, only now seeing just how awkward she is.

It's great.

ME: It's Emma. I'm sitting behind you.

Her phone lights up. After she reads it, she swivels in her chair, silently laughing before going back to her phone. When mine vibrates in my hand, I look down, chuckling under my breath.

BECKY: OH CRAP! Well, that's awkward.

ME: It's fine. LOL

She doesn't reply because Mr. Flint steps into the room, looking thunderous. "Sorry I'm late. I got stuck in traffic. Does everyone have their books?"

Without being asked, I pull mine out, not wanting to draw his attention to me. He already shows me a little more attention than I'd like him to. Pissing him off will just give him more ammunition. I finish setting my notebook and pens out before sitting back and facing the front of the class. The hairs on the back of my neck stand on end when Mr. Flint stares me down.

I look away, feeling uncomfortable. I don't even relax when he begins going over our coursework, setting out rules and what he expects to be handed in. I write as quickly as I can, irritated whenever he keeps flicking the PowerPoint to the next screen, not giving us a chance to get it all down. He's the one who called us here, not the other way around.

He's getting to the end of the hour when he asks us to copy down the points shown on the screen.

I'm so engrossed in getting it down so I can get home, that I don't see him walking up the aisle until I feel him standing next to me. His presence has the same effect on my body as it's had from our very first encounter. My mind, body and heart don't trust him. Every nerve is screaming at me to run. I've spent a long time doubting my instincts. I'd run at the smallest of conflicts or situations that took me out of my comfort zone. With Mr. Flint, it's like a switch has been flicked and I know what I'm feeling inside, know I can trust it.

"I looked over the paper you handed in to my substitute last week. I'd like to go over some things that I think need improving."

I glance around the room warily, seeing no one is paying attention to him. I don't look at him, feeling sick to my stomach as I keep working.

"I'm sorry, Mr. Flint, but it will have to be tomorrow before class. I have to get home as soon as class is finished."

I feel the air around us shift. Anger is pouring from him. When I glance at him from the corner of my eye, I notice his clenched hands and the veins bulging in his arms. I gulp, feeling my leg start to bounce.

"Emma, I don't think you're understanding me. If you want the passing grade on your work, you need to put time into it. When I tell you I need to talk about it to you privately, I mean it. If this class is getting too much for you, I can speak to the board and have you removed."

Fear snakes it way through my body as I turn to look at him. "Mr. Flint, I understand what you're saying, but I'm only scheduled for the hours applied. I apply those hours and I'm never late. The day I had off last week, I more than made up for," I tell him, trying to keep calm, and not panic.

"Do I make you nervous?" he asks, leaning over my desk, his face inches from mine. I flinch, moving away. He chuckles quietly under his breath, stepping closer. His runs his finger down my cheek, then over to move my hair behind my shoulder.

I grit my teeth, my breathing harsh and heavy. "So, what is it to be, Emma?"

"I'll kindly ask you to take a step back." My voice is filled with nerves, and he doesn't miss it, smiling like a cat that caught a fish.

"Ah, Emma, you really shouldn't argue back to a member of staff."

He moves away, heading back to the front of the class. "Hey, guys, due to some work that needs to be done on this floor, class tomorrow will be cancelled. I will send an email with a reading for you to do until our next lesson. I will see you Wednesday. Have a great weekend."

Feeling relief that I won't have to see him, I grab my stuff and shove it inside my bag. I'm not naïve; I know speaking up will most likely get him fired or suspended. What has me not running straight home to leave a message to the university is the fact I have no proof. None of the other students in my class are treated the same, and none of them pay attention when he's near me. They don't see what he does or hear what he says. It will be my word against his. And who would take the word of a girl who has spent years in a comatose state over the word of a respectable teacher who has worked for the university for a while? No one.

I pass Becky on my way out, her voice calling out to me slowing me down. She's still putting her things away when I turn around, well aware that Mr. Flint is watching me.

"Do you want a lift home?"

I shake my head, just wanting to get out of here. "No, thank you. I'm sorry I can't stick around. I really need to go."

She waves me off. "Text me for that coffee."

I force a smile before looking around the room, noticing there is just her and two male students left. Even before the feeling in the pit of my stomach hits, I decide to wait. Under no good conscience can I leave her with a pack of wolves. They'd eat her alive, and something tells me at least one of the three isn't afraid to attack.

"Actually, I'll walk out with you. Are you ready?" I ask, keeping an eye on the three men in the room. Mr. Flint watches me with an amused expression. I want to narrow my eyes at him, but I don't want to be held up any longer in this room with him. I'm going to have a serious talk with my department head, see if there is another teacher who teaches this class.

"Ready," she tells me, zipping her coat up. She doesn't notice the leering eyes on her, or if she does, she doesn't acknowledge it, not even saying goodbye as we leave the classroom.

"Can I ask you something that might seem strange?"

I give her a side glance, biting my lip. "Of course. What is it?"

"You know when you meet someone, can you tell if they're good or bad people?"

I wish I had that power.

"I'd like to think so, but so many people can hide their true intentions, and you won't know until it's too late."

"Yeah, but have you ever met someone or had someone stare at you and got instant chills?"

I give her a sharp glance, afraid someone has made her feel like that. "Yes, I have. Once or twice. Why? Has someone made you feel uncomfortable?"

She glances over her shoulder, down the dimly lit corridor, before facing me, her lips in a tight pout. "Yeah. It could just be me; I don't read people well. I've had people laugh *at* me, not with me, and I can't tell when someone is being sarcastic or not."

I stop her before we step outside, needing to know. It's just a feeling and a guess, but I think I'm right. "Becky, are you talking about Mr. Flint?"

Her startled eyes reach mine, before warily looking behind her. "What do you mean? Has he done something to you?"

"He did something to you?" I screech, wincing and lowering my tone. "Are you okay?"

She looks panicked when she takes my arm. "Shush, they might hear you. And no. But he makes me nervous. He asked me to stay behind after our second lesson, and I did. We were alone for a few seconds, but he put his hand on my thigh, rubbing me. Another girl from class walked in and I shot up from my seat. I tried to talk to our department head about it, but she basically told me it was my word against his. I tried to tell her I wasn't lying, that he creeped me out, but she put it down to me failing the class. Apparently, his family donate a lot to the university."

I feel sick at what I'm hearing.

"I'm so sorry, Becky. I think we need to go to someone higher if she isn't listening to us. Money isn't a reason to let someone sexually harass us."

"He's done it to you?"

I nod sharply. "He's always getting in my personal space, always touching me inappropriately. He's tried more than once to get me to stay behind. He did it just now in class. But like you, it will be my word against his."

"I understand. I don't want his behaviour to affect my learning. If this goes to the schoolboard, and they make us leave until it's resolved, that's my money and time wasted. I didn't know he was doing it to other girls. What should we do?"

I can understand her reasoning. It's a hard situation to be in, especially when he's the one in power.

"I don't know, but if he's done it to us, maybe more girls will come forward."

She scoffs, rolling her eyes. "If you're thinking of asking around, don't bother. I got my head bit off by one girl. She slept with him willingly, and when I mentioned what he did, she told me I was jealous and that they are in love with each other."

"It's not all of us he's doing it to, then," I say, sickened. He shouldn't be sleeping with a student, anyway, even if she is of age. He's abusing his position.

"Nope. I was actually going to tell my dad if he did it again, but since then, he's left me alone."

"I'll think of something and text you. There must be a way to get proof to the schoolboard. They won't be able to make excuses for his actions then. He'd never be able to get away with it."

"Ooh, I like where this is going. I love Veronica Mars, and this sounds right up her alley."

"Veronica who?" I ask.

She shakes her head at me, looking utterly appalled. "You don't know who Veronica Mars is?"

I shake my head. "Nope."

"You've not lived. Go home, watch it online, and let me know what you think. Unless you hate it, then keep it to yourself."

I laugh at her bluntness. "I will," I tell her, then turn to the empty corridor behind us, a shiver running down my spine. "Let's go before they come out. We've been out here long enough."

"I'll speak to you soon," Becky tells me, before we step outside.

I open my umbrella up, waving goodbye to Becky as she turns left and I walk right. It's darker now, but a few of the streetlamps are still not on.

A sense of foreboding washes over me when the back of my neck starts to burn. I check out my surroundings, squinting into the darkness and seeing nothing.

I turn back around, my foot in the air to take another step, when I hear a can being kicked behind me. Alarmed and panicked, I rush forward, needing to get out of the dark pathway and into a crowded area. They still haven't caught the killer, which only has me running. I look over my shoulder to check that someone isn't chasing me and see nothing, yet… I still feel their eyes on me.

I bump into a hard body when I reach the corner, and I cry out, ready to yell for help. My umbrella falls to the floor as I open my mouth. Strong hands grip my biceps, causing the scream that was ready to burst free, to freeze in panic.

Flashes of Darren hitting me surface. I never want to go through that kind of pain ever again, to not know if I'll come out breathing or not.

"Emma, what the fuck! What's happened? Why are you walking down here in the dark by yourself?"

I fall forward, my head hitting Banner's chest as I hold onto him for comfort. "I'm sorry. I panicked." He bends down to pick up my umbrella, passing it to me. "Thank you."

"Why did you panic?" he asks, pulling me close.

I'm not going to tell him about Mr. Flint; Banner will only go back in there and start a fight. I don't want him to be kicked out of uni because of that sleaze ball.

"It was dark, I was alone, and it felt like someone was watching me," I tell him, missing out the part I was already freaked out by: Mr. Flint.

He stops mid-step, looking around the dimly lit courtyard. "I don't see anyone," he says, before we continue to walk. "Why were you coming out of the side door, anyway? I've been waiting out here for nearly twenty minutes for you to get out."

"They're doing maintenance or something. Oh, and before I forget, I don't have class tomorrow now. It got cancelled due to the work that needs to be done."

He grins. "More time together, then."

Becky flashes through my mind, and I nearly jump in the air when I tell him. "I made a friend today."

Banner knows what a big deal this is to me, knowing how closed off I am. The proud look on his face when I tell him disappears though, and I look around, thinking he saw something.

"Please tell me they're female."

I hide my grin against his bicep at the way he sounded when he said it. "She is. Her name is Becky. In fact, she gave us a new TV show to check out. It's called Veronica Mars. Have you seen it?"

His body relaxes next to me. "Yeah, it's about a hot chick who kicks the arse of everyone who messes with her."

"Want to watch it with me?"

We pause at the car park, and he turns to face me, tilting my chin up so he can see me. "I'd watch that PS. I Love you if it meant spending time with you."

His words do things to my body that I don't understand. This is another moment I will lock away, so I can remember it forever.

I can't look away from him, stuck in a trance of lust and desire. I unconsciously sway forward, my eyes drooping at the look he gives me.

A car honking nearby has us pulling away, the moment between us breaking. He grunts something under his breath.

"Did you say something?"

"I said, let's go get popcorn." He smiles, opening the car door for me.

I watch as he moves around the front of the car, his lips moving like he's talking to himself. I look away, out of the window. I want him to want me. One minute I think he's hot for me, the next, I feel like he sees me as a sister or one of the guys. Not that he talks about girls to me. He actually keeps that part of his life private.

As he gets in, my eyes catch a shadow moving in the trees near the path to the English building, and instantly, I'm alert and uneasy. I sit up, moving forward in my seat to get a better look, but before I can point out the moving shadow to Banner, it disappears like it wasn't even there. I blink, scanning the area for any sign of him, but don't see anything.

Every instinct in my body is screaming at me of the danger. I feel like I'm being hunted, like prey waiting to be slaughtered.

As we head out of the carpark, we drive past Mr. Flint, who is standing next to his car, his door open and ready to get in. When he sees me, he grins, before saluting me. I look away, turning my attention to the road.

I know I'm going to have to tell Banner about him sooner or later, but not right now. I just hope he doesn't get mad when he finds out I've kept something from him.

Chapter 9

After a night of restless sleep, I'm struggling to pick my feet up. Lake and her boyfriend, Max, are due here any moment. I'm tired, cranky, but also excited to see my best friend.

"We're going to head out to give you some privacy," Mark says, as he grabs his car keys and coat.

"You don't need to go. This is your home," I tell him, guilt twisting my stomach at him feeling like he needs to leave.

"It's yours, too," he says, frowning. "We're going to grab a late breakfast, then head out to meet up with some friends for a birthday."

"I know it is." I hate seeing the hurt look on his face. This has been the first time I've felt at home in a while. "And if you're sure. I don't have class tonight, so I'll see you later."

He leans over to kiss my cheek, Levi coming to do the same to my other. I giggle, swatting them both away.

"We'll see you later," Levi tells me, winking.

I smile back, watching them leave before running to the bathroom and banging on the door. "Hurry up, they're going to be here any minute," I shout to Banner. We got up late due to me tossing and turning. Banner tried to get me to talk about what was bothering me, but I couldn't tell him about Mr. Flint, or the feeling I keep getting that someone is watching me.

"Finished," he shouts, before I hear the tap turn off. Seconds later, the door opens, and he walks out wiping his mouth on a towel, grinning at me. "Stop stressing. It's going to be fine. It's Lake, for Christ sakes. You two were joint at the hip."

We were. "But that was years ago. Now, we're practically strangers. I'm nervous—and I want her boyfriend to like me. She loves him."

He takes my hand, pulling me away from the bathroom and into the front room. "First of all, years could pass between you and you'll still meet up and act like you saw each other yesterday. Friendship like that doesn't just end. Not real friendship, anyway. Secondly, who gives a shit if her boyfriend does or doesn't like you. It should be him worrying about you liking him. Stop panicking over nothing."

I take a deep breath, trying to calm my nerves. "I'll try. Do you want another cup of coffee?"

He grimaces. "Uh, no. And I think you should lay off for a while," he says, glancing down at my feet.

I stop tapping my foot on the carpet, wincing. "Yeah, maybe that last cup wasn't such a good idea."

He throws his head back and laughs. "You think?"

There's a knock on the door that has us both pausing, our heads snapping towards the source of the noise. "They're here," I whisper from the side of my mouth.

"So, answer the door," he whispers back, not moving.

Another knock.

"Okay," I whisper back.

"Why are we whispering?"

I look over my shoulder as I go to open the door, shrugging. "In case they hear us?"

He chuckles, stepping closer as I open the door. What greets me comes as a surprise. I had expected Lake and her boyfriend, but instead, standing in front of me are two beautiful little girls, bouncing on the soles of their feet, two god-like men, and a beautiful woman... then a familiar face.

Lake waves, throwing her bright smile at me, and I relax.

A tug on my top has me looking down at a little girl with long, brown ringlets. "Please may we use your toilet? I really need to pee, and so does Lily. Pretty please?" she asks, holding her hands together.

Amused and slightly baffled, I slowly nod. "It's that door over there," I tell her, pointing her in the right direction. The beautiful little girl takes Lily's hand, dragging her over to the bathroom.

"I'll go first because I've waited the longest."

Lily doesn't say anything, letting her drag her away. When I glance back at Lake, she's smiling.

"It was a long car ride and they've needed to pee every five minutes," Lake explains, as I gesture for them to come in.

"And drink every two," a dark-haired lad says, rolling his eyes. Lake elbows him, and he grunts. When his eyes land on me, a mischievous grin spreads across his face. He steps forward as I take one back, but he's fast. A light squeal passes my lips when he picks me up in his arms and swings me around.

"I'm so happy to meet you," he tells me, holding me tight. "Lake has talked about you non-stop, so I feel like we're already best friends."

He puts me down and I gape at him. He really isn't shy. My eyes travel to Lake, ignoring the chuckles coming from the others in their group.

"This is Max, my boyfriend," she tells me, rolling her eyes as if to say, 'what can I do?'.

I wave lamely. "Hey, nice to meet you."

"You won't be saying that later," the other man says, this one older and sporting many tattoos. He's not as covered as Banner, from what I can see, but he's got his fair share. He's built, all muscle, like Max, yet he carries it differently—more intimidating. He exudes power, but when he notices me glancing his way, his smile completely transforms his face, and I begin to relax somewhat. "I'm Maverick, Max's brother. This is my wife, Teagan."

"It's nice to meet you," I tell him.

The bathroom door opens and both girls come running out. The one with dark ringlets goes to her mother, but the quiet girl with golden locks—Lily—goes straight to Maverick.

I feel Max watching me from the corner of my eye, so I look up, hoping I didn't space out and ignore someone.

"This is Lily," he says, answering my silent question. He gestures to the blonde cuddling Maverick's leg and I wave at her. "She's my sister-niece, and the other troublemaker is Faith, my niece."

"Sister-niece?" I ask, utterly confused, looking between the group. The woman they called Teagan, smiles, looking away.

"She's technically their sister, but Maverick and Teagan adopted her. They're still getting used to what to call her."

I feel Banner press against my back. "Can't choose between the cool uncle or the protective brother?"

Max looks Banner over with a sceptical eye. "Did someone run out of paper, dude?"

My eyes widen as I choke on laughter. Lake groans, hitting him in the stomach again.

Banner's chest rumbles against my back. "Yeah. That and I like the pain," he says, making Max's eyes go wide.

"I can't believe you said that," Lake hisses at Max, before turning to Banner. "How are you, Banner?"

"Still breathing." He shrugs, before stepping around me. "I wondered when you would notice me."

He pulls her in for a hug, and Max clears his throat loudly, his eyes bugging out at Banner. I giggle, watching with amusement as Banner pulls back, tucking me into his side. Max does the same with Lake, never taking his eyes off Banner.

"Chill. Me and Lake are friends. We've never dated, kissed, or anything. You can stop trying to kill me in your mind."

I gape at Banner being so blunt. Maverick, on the other hand, finds it amusing and bursts out laughing. "You'll be fine, kid. Just don't feed his ego. We have to fit him back in the car if we want to get home."

Max looks affronted when he faces his brother. "If he wants to lick my ego, let him. Lake is forever making me feel worthless. It needs the boost."

"Stop being a drama queen," Lake tells him, biting back a smile.

He kisses the side of her head, and Faith makes a face. "Eww. Would you stop kissing! You're just like Mummy and Daddy. It's gross. Isn't it, Lily?"

We all giggle, but I notice Lily doesn't answer. She just nods, her face turning pink at the attention.

"Lake said you were spending the day at the zoo. Are you excited?" I ask them.

Lily's eyes light up like it's Christmas morning. "Yes!" Her voice is soft, angel-like.

"We're going to see some big bears," Faith adds, her voice filled with excitement.

Max gives her a funny look. "They don't have bears."

She puts her hands on her hips. "Yes, they do! And they have lions and tigers."

Max looks up at her father. "You been watching the Wizard of Oz again?"

Maverick sighs, rolling his eyes. "Yes. She loves anything with animals in."

Faith draws my attention again when she puffs her chest out. "Animals love me, and I love them. When I'm older, I'm going to have millions."

"Not in my house," Maverick mutters under his breath.

"But, Dad!" she whines.

Lily just watches them both, a small smile on her lips, but I can see the hesitancy in her eyes. I want to ask how they came about adopting her, but it seems too personal.

"Let's go to the zoo," Teagan tells them cheerfully.

Maverick relaxes when his daughter's narrowed eyes turn to focus on her mum. "Can Lake's friend come?"

"What about me?" Banner blurts out.

She looks over her shoulder, eyeing him up and down, making me giggle. "I think you'll scare the animals away. Me and Lily are excited."

Banner pouts like it's a real issue, and I have to look away when he finds me chuckling silently.

"It was lovely to meet you," Teagan says, as she takes her daughters' hand.

"It was nice to meet you all, too. I hope I get to see you again soon."

"And me; you can play with my Barbies," Faith tells me, and I smile wide at her, winking.

Maverick turns to his brother, a stern look on his face. "No getting into trouble. I'm not staying overnight just so I can bail you out in the morning. You'd better be here when we get back," he tells him.

My eyes widen, looking at Lake. She catches my eye and blushes, looking away. "I already told you I didn't mean to ruin our holiday. The lad touched Lake's" he pauses, looking down at the girls, wincing, "A.R.S.E."

"I'm not getting into this," Maverick tells him, before turning to me and Banner. "Don't let him have anything fizzy and try to keep his sweet intake to a minimum."

When he takes Lily's hand and they turn to leave, I look between Max and Lake, trying to work out if he's serious or not. Max whistles, eyeing the ceiling like there's something amazing there, and Lake looks down at her feet.

Mine and Banner's eyes meet, and we widen them, both silently saying, 'what the fuck'. Surely, he can't be that bad.

I mean, what could he possibly get up to in four hours.

∼

"I can't believe they don't include starters in the all you can eat," Max whines as we step outside of the car.

We all narrow our eyes at him, slamming our car doors. "Don't, Max. I'm still pissed you got us banned from another restaurant."

"He's done this before?" Banner asks, chuckling. He found the whole ordeal amusing from the beginning. I, on the other hand, couldn't have been more embarrassed. And yes, kind of amused.

Lake looks at him over the car roof. "You'll be surprised. It was easier to ask him where he *could* go rather than have him tell me the places he'd been banned from ever stepping foot in again. The list was never ending. We can't even get takeout anymore because he complains about portion sizes or missing food."

"I'm not that bad," Max scoffs.

"Max, you're lucky they didn't call the police. You pushed the waiter over," Lake warns him heatedly. She didn't seem surprised by his actions though, didn't even seem embarrassed. Something tells me he's done worse stuff in her company than the incident that just occurred.

"Lake," he whines slowly, throwing his arm over the back of her shoulders. "It was an accident. I thought he was going to punch me in the face. I can't have him ruining the merchandise." He gestures to his face, ignoring Lake as she rolls her eyes.

"So, you pushed him over?" I ask, stopping outside the restaurant we're going in—we're hoping the second try will be the charm.

He gives me an eye roll. "I didn't push him. I got up too fast and he got too close. It was automatic reflexes. And does no one care he was gonna hit me?"

"You told him to go back to school and learn how to read the fine print," I remind him.

"And teased him about his trousers being too tight," Lake adds.

"His boner was staring at me—straight in the eye," he groans, looking up at the sky.

Banner chuckles, wrapping his arm around my shoulder and pulling me to his side. "Max is right about that. Every time he came back from the table with the group of girls, it got bigger."

Max looks at him, his eyes bright with amusement. "And the wet patch... I nearly told him I'd pay him to take a break, get it sorted."

Banner nods but remains quiet.

"Emma," a feminine voice calls from behind me. We spin around, and I beam when I find Jordan walking towards us, a smile spread across her face.

"Hey, Jordan. How are you?"

"I'm good. You okay to meet up next week?"

Shit. "I'm so sorry. I forgot to text you. I actually have to meet up with someone else Friday before class," I tell her, feeling my face heat. I don't want any of them here to know who I'm going to meet. I know they wouldn't judge me, but I don't want Jordan knowing my personal business just yet. I don't know if I can trust her.

She frowns, looking disappointed. "Oh no. I was looking forward to catching up with you. Message me when you're free next, there was something I needed to talk to you about."

She looks serious about it. I wish I had booked Milly for another day, but I've got too much work to catch up on in the week, and coursework.

"I will. It will have to be the week after. I've got a lot on."

"That's fine. Mum said you're making cakes for their bake sale. Did you want me to come and help?"

I nod. "That would be great. I'll need help protecting the cakes from Banner. He'll end up eating them all."

"Cakes?" Max says. I glance at him, smiling when he gets a dazed look in his eyes and licks his lips.

"Let me know a day," she says, her eyes twinkling at Max's behaviour.

Banner clears his throat, and I jump, flushing as I realise I haven't made any introductions. "Jordan, this is Banner, my friend I was telling you about." Banner tenses beside me, and when I look to see what's wrong, his jaw is clenched and he's looking away. Okay, then. "This is Lake, my best friend from school. She's come down for a visit"

"And I'm Max, the best-looking man you'll ever meet," he tells her, winking.

"You're not my type," Jordan tells him slowly, narrowing her eyes at him. She looks at his arm wrapped around Lake, and her lip curls.

I giggle at Max's expression. He looks wounded, like someone told him he couldn't eat his favourite food.

"I'm everyone's type," he tells her, sounding a little screechy.

"Lower the tone," Lake whispers from the side of her mouth.

"You're shit out of luck anyway. There's only one me, and I'm spoken for." He snubs his nose at her, and I begin to think he's really hurt by what she said.

"Do you have a vagina?" Jordan blurts out, raising her eyebrow at him.

When Max looks down at his crotch area, I have to hide my face in Banner's arm to smother my laughter.

"Do you really want to see my appendage?"

"I think she's trying to tell you she's into girls," Lake tells him, trying to hide her amusement.

Still looking confused, he eyes his girlfriend, then Jordan. "So do I, but what does that have to do with the price of chips?"

Jordan rolls her eyes, sighing. "I'm gay. Lesbian. Now you can stop panicking over the possibility a girl who likes dick, doesn't like *you*."

He grins, showing his pearly whites. "If I didn't love my girlfriend, I'd have you changing your mind."

She groans. "You remind me of someone I know."

"There's only one me, babe."

Jordan shakes her head at him before looking to Lake. "You two together?"

"Yes. He can be a bit much, but he grows on you."

"Like vegetables?" Jordan asks through chuckles.

Laughing, Lake nods. "I like you."

"I like you, too. But I admire you more for putting up with him."

"Hey," Max snaps. "I'm a fucking legend. Let's go, Lake. I don't want her filling your head with stuff. And vegetables? I'm chocolate, baby. I melt on your tongue, and once you have a piece of me, you want more."

"Until you eat too much and throw up, vowing to never touch the stuff again," Jordan tells him teasingly, before facing me. "Text me. I need to go; I'm meeting some friends inside." She glances at the others. "It was nice meeting you all."

"You too," Banner and Lake tell her.

Max pouts, glaring at the door Jordan just walked through. "I don't like her."

We all laugh at his expression, heading inside the restaurant. I spot Jordan sitting with a group of friends, but the minute I notice a pretty brunette watching me, I look away.

"The food here good?" Max asks as he sits down.

"Their burgers are the best in Whithall."

"I'll get two, then. I'm starved," Max says, rubbing his stomach.

"I wouldn't, mate. I can barely eat one."

Max looks at him with a challenge. "Trust me. I bet I could eat three." He sighs dramatically. "But I promised Lake I wouldn't eat like a starved animal."

I have no idea how big their burgers are, as this is the first time I've eaten here, but from what Banner told me, they are huge, with loads of toppings. And if he struggles with one, then I believe him when he tells Max not to order two.

When Banner goes to argue, Lake butts in. "I wouldn't bother. I can tell you right now he's going to bet you money that he can, and you'll lose. He's a dustbin. He can eat anything and everything put in front of him."

"All right, then," Banner says, watching Max glance over the menu hungrily.

I pull off my coat when it gets too warm and throw it around the back of my chair. When I sit back down, Lake takes my wrist in her hands.

"Oh, my God, you got a tattoo?"

I smile at her shocked expression. "I did. Yesterday, actually."

She looks up from my wrist, her eyes soft. "It's beautiful."

"Thank you," I tell her, swallowing past the lump in my throat. Max glances over, and from the look in his eyes, I can tell he knows what the tattoo means and who Lara is. He doesn't say anything, but rather conveys his approval with a chin lift.

"Did it hurt?"

I shake my head. "No. It just felt like tiny cat scratches to be honest. Some bits were sharper than others."

Max scoffs and my eyes go to him. "You've never been scratched by a fucking cat if that's what you're comparing it to."

Before I can open my mouth, Lake turns to him, snapping, "Will you stop whining about Thor. You're being a baby."

Max's eyes nearly bug out of his head, and instead of answering Lake, he turns to me and Banner and pulls up the sleeves of his top. His arms are covered in red scratches, some looking worse than others.

"I look like I've been self-harming. The old lady who works at the corner shop told me I could go to her if I ever felt that alone again," he tells us, and I bite my lip to stop myself from laughing. "The fucking rat hates me. I've even had to get a 'beware of the cat' sign made for us because it attacked the postman the other day. He was gonna sue us. I know it."

"Stop being dramatic," Lake orders, struggling not to laugh. "Thor is amazing. You must piss him off."

"I piss Splinter off? That fucking rat has gone for my balls more times than you do when you've had a cider."

"I wish you would stop calling him that," Lake snaps, her face turning bright red. I choke on laughter, finding the two highly amusing. I haven't laughed like this since before Lara. It's clear she loves him. No one who didn't would be able to handle his behaviour. As entertaining as it is, he must be stressful at times.

"I'm confused. Are we talking about a cat or a rat?" Banner asks.

"A cat," Lake says, at the same time Max says, "Rat."

Lake turns, narrowing her eyes at her boyfriend. "I wish you would stop saying he's a rat."

"Splinter?" I ask, trying to think where I've heard that name before.

Banner suddenly starts laughing. "Oh, my fucking god," he says, trying to catch his breath. "From the Ninja Turtles?"

Max grins, nodding. "Yep. Fucking thing looks and acts like him too. Sneaky little bastard."

Lake ignores him and faces me, rolling her eyes. "Did your nan tell you she saw us at Lexington's German market?"

"No, she didn't. Did she go with Granddad or a group of friends?"

Lake grins. "A group of friends. They were checking out the foods. I didn't even realise it was her at first. I was eating some Bangladeshi food that they were giving out for free, Max started screaming, and that's when I saw her."

"He started screaming?"

"Yeah. At first, I thought he saw a spider, but when I saw your nan and her friends, I walked over. One of her friends had pinched his bum."

"Fucking bruised too," Max says, never looking away from the menu.

I giggle. I can only imagine what they were up to. Unless their husbands are with them, they don't behave.

"I bet she fussed over you when she saw you."

My nan loves Lake. When my parents would send me to my grandparents' house, Lake would often stay with me.

"She did. I didn't think she was going to let me go. It was good seeing her. I wish your granddad was there. When was the last time you saw them?"

I think it over, wincing. "A while ago. Nan had her gallbladder removed about four months ago, so Granddad couldn't come get me. I was gonna catch the train up there, but they wouldn't let me. Then I had to move here. I guess time got away with me."

"They'll understand. They love you. How's Mark? Still going to the gym?"

I start laughing. "He's good. And he owns one now."

"We're gonna go order food while you talk," Banner interrupts, whispering. I go to grab my purse, but his hand stops me. "I'll buy it."

I look up, feeling warmth rush through me. "Thank you."

He winks before getting to his feet.

"You gonna buy mine, too?"

Banner looks him over. "Nah, you aren't as pretty as Emma."

Max scoffs, muttering something to Banner as they walk off.

"You look so happy, Lake. I really like him."

Her eyes go soft as she flicks them over my shoulder to where the lads are. "I am. But enough about me; I want to hear about you. What is going on between you and Banner? And can I add, how fit has he got! He was always good-looking in school, but Jesus, now it's hard to look at him."

I blush, shaking my head in amusement. Banner was hot before, but as he's grown, he's gotten better-looking. He's like a fine wine.

"There's nothing going on between us," I squeak. "What's made you say that?"

She gives me a look that says, 'yeah right'. "First of all, he can't stop touching you. When Max hugged you, I thought his jaw was gonna snap. And the way he looks at you It's like he's seeing colour for the first time. There's no way you are just friends, because you look at him the same way, only you're more discreet about it."

My neck and cheeks heat at her observation. Can he tell I have the hots for him? Oh god, what if he knows I'm secretly in love with him?

"He doesn't like me that way. Trust me. He's just a friend. He was there for me through it all, Lake. He saw it. There's no way he would want someone as weak as me for a girlfriend. You forget, I knew the girls he slept with in high school. They were sexy, confident, outgoing—everything I'm not."

Her expression is filled with pity and I have to glance away. "Emma, you are so much more than you give yourself credit for. He's in love with you."

"He's not."

She looks over my shoulder before glancing back at me. "He is. But something tells me you'll find out soon enough."

I won't.

Banner and Max join us back at the table. Max begins to fill in the silence, but I can't concentrate long enough to listen. I can't get Lake's words out of my head. Could she be right? Could Banner really have feelings for me, or is she mistaking his feelings for me as a friend for something more?

I guess there's only one way to find out. I'm just not sure that I've got the courage to gamble everything in order to find the answer.

Chapter 10

The bark pressing against my back makes it hard to get comfortable. I keep shifting around, trying to find a spot I'm happy with. Once I'm out of the way of a lone stick digging into my spine, I pull the blanket I'm sharing with Banner, tighter around me, sighing happily. I snuggle into Banner's side with my cup of hot chocolate in hand.

"People are looking at us like we're nuts," I tell him, closing my eyes briefly at the sound of rain hitting our umbrella—if you can call it that; it's big enough to cover a tent.

Banner's head shifts, and without looking, I know he's gazing down at me. "We are nuts. We're sitting in the park when it's freezing cold and raining."

"At least it's not snowing," I tease, at least grateful for that. "And this was your idea."

"You love the rain."

"I love a lot of things."

"Oh yeah? Tell me some," he says, his voice light with amusement.

I inwardly roll my eyes when a woman walks past, looking at us like we're something she wiped off her shoe.

When she's out of hearing range, I giggle. "Did you see her face?"

He scoffs. "Couldn't miss it. With the way she was looking, you'd think we were sitting on her front doorstep."

"Why are we here, again?"

"You said you wanted to see the park."

"When it's not raining," I tell him.

"Do you want to go?"

"No!" I tell him quickly, before he decides to pack up. Once I realise how desperate I sound, I clear my throat. "I mean, no. It's not like we're getting wet. Much. And we have three blankets around us, and we're sitting on a plastic mat."

"Don't forget the legendary umbrella."

I laugh when I look at the umbrella he's dug into the ground between our legs, so it doesn't blow over. When he pulled it out of the car, I thought he'd lost his mind. He's lucky it's not as windy as it was last night, or he would be saying bye-bye to it.

"Where did you get it?"

"Mum left it the last time she came to watch a game."

"When is your next game?"

"Not until spring."

I rest my head on his shoulder, looking out at the park. Even dreary and wet the place looks beautiful. I wish I could draw, because there's a little girl holding her mother's hand, wearing bright yellow rain boots and splashing in puddles. It's a beautiful sight to see; something I wish I had memories of as a child.

I must have sighed because Banner places his hand on my leg. "You okay?"

Still watching the little girl, I answer him. "I wish I had that as a child."

I feel his gaze look her way. "Splashing in puddles?"

"Yeah. I used to lie in bed all the time thinking of something, *anything*, to remember a time when my parents loved me. I remember them sitting through Lara's plays and clapping, I remember them taking her ice-skating for her thirteenth birthday, but not once do I remember something they did with me. I'd have wished for anything to cherish. Even a moment of splashing in puddles. But I don't have one. After Lara, and then Darren attacking me, I tried to find reasons as to why I should love them. They're my parents, and I do care for them—I'll be sad if something were to happen to them—but I've stopped feeling love for them. They're strangers to me now."

He pulls me tighter against him, kissing the top of my head. I close my eyes, forcing the tears threatening at bay.

"Emma, your parents fucked up when it came to you. I know you don't want to hear it, but your sister wasn't perfect. They treated her like a princess instead of disciplining her."

I give him a sharp look. "What are you trying to say?"

He drops the blanket and scrubs a hand down his face. "I don't want you to hate me. I don't want to lose you."

"You won't lose me," I tell him, feeling my throat tighten.

He looks doubtful, making me wary. "Lara did drugs before she got them off Darren. My mum caught her buying some in town and called your parents. They called my mum a liar, and the next day at school, Lara was flashing off a new phone and bragging about the clothes she had got."

My eyes widen when something registers. "Wait! I think that was the day they sent me off to my grandparents for the week, saying I was a bad influence on her. I was supposed to be with her that day she went into town, but I needed to go to the library to pick up some books. I got back, and they told me I had to go my grandparents."

He nods, looking grim. "I heard you were sent away. My mum tried talking to them a few times. Lara was always drunk or high. I think your parents ignoring it did more damage to her. They neglected the both of you. With her, they chose to shower her with affection, when really, she needed some tough loving. And with you, they just ignored you, when you deserved to be showered with affection."

My eyes water at hearing him talk about Lara that way. "I didn't know she did drugs. I was close to her, and I would have noticed."

"No, you wouldn't have. I didn't know your sister well enough to say whether rumours were true or not, but she wasn't perfect, Em. If I were to guess, she hid it from you well. She needed someone who didn't lecture her to come off them. I know a few of her mates tried to get her to get help, but she wouldn't listen."

"I feel like I didn't know her, Banner," I whisper, feeling a sharp pain in my chest. "This is hard to process. I want to hate you for slagging her off when she isn't here to defend herself, to yell at you for talking bad of her, but I don't have it in me. The months leading up to her death was when I knew something was going on. I was blinded before because I craved her affection. She was the only one who showed me any at home. Outside, I had Lake and her family. I just wish she'd come to me for help. I hate myself for not seeing what was going on with her."

"I think, in the end, she didn't know herself."

"In her diary, she was fine—up until a few months before. That was when she started ranting over Darren. I didn't know it was him she was writing about, but she said she loved him, that he was the only one who got her. It got worse in the weeks before she died. He wouldn't leave his girlfriend."

"It was a messed-up situation," he whispers.

"Those drugs were mixed with poison. Whether she or Darren knew that when he gave them to her, I don't know. Either way, she killed herself. She's not coming back. She left me and didn't even say goodbye."

"Come on," he says, jumping to his feet and knocking the umbrella over. I scream when the rain hits me in the face and glare up at Banner. He pulls me up, letting the blankets and sheet get drenched.

"What are you doing?"

"I didn't come here to make you sad. I came here to cheer you up."

"Okay" I say slowly, scrunching my eyebrows together.

"Jump."

"Jump?"

His smile is contagious. "Yep. You want happy memories, then jump. Splash in the puddles to your heart's content. Jump!"

Holding hands, we move over to the path. I jump in the air, splashing in a puddle, getting soaked. I let him go, giggling as I kick the puddle, splashing rain water everywhere. I feel free for the first time in ages. The rain splatters across my face as I look up into the sky, my eyes closed. I spread my arms wide, spinning around in circles, laughing.

There's no almost free about this moment. Not one thing. All my troubles, all my fears, they wash away with the rain.

Hands grab my hips and I stumble to a stop. Opening my eyes, I meet Banner's honey-coloured gaze. Everything around me stills, the world gone quiet as we stare into each other's eyes.

"Banner," I whisper, feeling like this is the moment. The moment I tell him how I feel.

He takes a step forward, his chest caressing mine as he looks down at me. The desire staring back at me takes my breath away.

He tucks a wet strand of hair behind my ear before running the back of his hand down my cheek. I lean into his touch, following the warmth of it, and close my eyes.

When I open them, his fingers press into my hips, and he leans forward. I hold my breath, my heart beating rapidly.

He's going to kiss me.

Just as I pucker my lips, ready to meet him halfway, his head jerks forward, smacking into mine.

"Ow," I moan, holding my sore head.

He glares at someone over his shoulder before bending down and picking up a football. "Go fucking play somewhere else," he growls, kicking the football back before turning back to me. "Who fucking plays football in the rain?"

I try to hide my grin but fail. "Um, the same kind of people who sit in the rain to drink coffee?"

He chuckles, rubbing the back of his neck. My phone rings in my pocket and I shrug apologetically when Banner curses under his breath. I pull it out, seeing Mark's name on the screen.

"Hey, Mark, what's up?"

"Are you coming home for dinner? It's ready."

Shit, I forgot he was cooking us a Sunday dinner today. He would have done it tomorrow, but he has someone going to the gym to inspect the new sauna he had fitted.

"Yes. We're on our way right now, Mark."

Banner grins, leaning forward. "She's lying. We're still in the park."

I narrow my eyes at him. "We can leave now."

"Why are you two in the park? It's pissing down with rain," Mark tells me, like I didn't already know.

"Because we're weird. We won't be long—ten minutes at the most."

"See you then," he says, before ending the call.

Sliding my phone back into my pocket, I glare at Banner. "Why did you tell him I was lying? Everyone says they're on their way, even if they haven't left yet."

He just keeps grinning. "No one lies to Mark in front of me."

"You got that off a Facebook meme, didn't you?"

He nods. "Yeah, but I didn't think Mark would appreciate been called Suzie."

I just laugh and shake my head, walking over to pick the blankets up. "Come on, you tattletale. Let's get back and dry off. Do you have spare clothes?"

"Yeah. I've been keeping a few bits at yours, but I brought another bag."

I sigh and stop what I'm doing to face him. "You do realise I'm okay. You don't have to stay with me all the time. You must be getting bored of being cooped up with me."

He looks hurt by my admission. "I like being there. The flat I share gets too rowdy and it drives me nuts. I can't even watch a movie. Plus, I like being with you. But if you want your space, just tell me and I can go back."

Warmth fills me at his honesty. "No. I like you being there. I just don't want you to get bored of me."

Something flashes in his eyes. "I could never get bored of you."

As he takes a step forward, my phone starts ringing again. He curses to the sky and I giggle. It's Mark ringing when I look at the screen, so I show it to Banner.

"This is why you should always lie to Suzie," I tease.

He laughs, throwing everything into a black bag since it needs to be rung out, then washed. "Let's get going before he drives down here."

We start off down the path, soaking wet. As we near the exit of the park, we stop to let a woman through. She tilts her umbrella back as she passes.

"Becky," I greet, surprised to see her. What a small world.

"Hey, Emma," she says slowly, raking her gaze over me, then doing the same to Banner, a confused look crossing her expression. "Um, why, if you've got an umbrella, do you two look like you've been swimming?"

I giggle when she begins to sound more confused.

"We were splashing in the puddles."

She laughs like she thinks we're joking. "Funny. But seriously, is there a huge puddle or something I should be warned about? I don't fancy getting too wet. This umbrella isn't helping much, and I need to get to the other side of the park to meet my dad."

"She's being serious," Banner says, looking away when he starts to chuckle at her expression.

I just smile. "It's a long story. Do you want us to give you a lift somewhere?"

"Um, no, thank you. I think I might be safer walking through the park. You two are kind of weird."

I don't take offence to her remark, since I can see she's said it as a fact, not maliciously. "We are. But you're safe with us."

"I'm good, thank you. I was actually wondering if you wanted to meet up next week before class on Friday."

"I can't on Friday, but I can Wednesday."

"Why can't you on Friday?"

"Nosey," Banner mutters.

I elbow him in the stomach for being rude. Fortunately, Becky doesn't seem to mind and instead just shrugs at him.

"Sorry. I told you I was socially awkward."

"It's fine. I have to meet up with someone before class."

"Is it about Mr. Flint? I can come."

"Mr. Flint?" Banner asks, stepping closer. "Isn't that your Historical Literature teacher?"

Sending Becky a look and a subtle shake of my head, I turn to Banner. "Yeah." I glance back at Becky, speaking before she can say anything else. "It's just someone I need to talk to about something. It's personal."

"Why would you want to talk about your teacher?"

I inwardly groan, not wanting to lie to him, but thankfully, Becky picks up on the tension and answers. "We want to talk to someone about the criteria this term. He's set too much work out for us to complete," she lies.

"Oh."

"Well, we'd better get going. My cousin is waiting to dish the dinner out. Are you sure you don't want a lift?"

"I'm good. Have a nice evening, though."

"Will do. And I'll text you a time and place for Wednesday, okay?"

"Sounds good."

We separate, both going our different ways. It's not until we exit the park that Banner speaks up. "She's the friend you made?"

"Yeah."

"Emma?"

"Yeah."

"I'm worried about you."

"What? Why?" I ask, turning to face him.

"She's really fucking weird."

I burst out laughing, tucking my arm under his and resting my head on his shoulder. Even freezing cold and soaked through, this has been the second-best day since my arrival at Whithall. My first one is always going to be the first time Banner fell asleep in bed with me.

~

We walk through the door and come to a sudden stop when we find Mark leaning on the back of the sofa, his ankles and arms crossed, a stern expression on his face.

"If you get a cold, don't blame me."

I roll my eyes at him. "I won't. I've already filled that spot."

His eyes flick to Banner, flashing with mirth. "Who?"

"Banner."

"What? Why me? I brought blankets," he argues, looking affronted. "And what about the puddles? Don't they count for something?"

My lips twist as I tap my chin, pretending to think about it. "Depends how bad this cold will get."

"Well, it's gonna get worse if you don't get in the shower and warm up," he urges, pushing me towards the bathroom.

I laugh. "Okay. You go shower in the bathroom, I'll use Mark and Levi's en-suite."

"Don't be long, otherwise this dinner will go dry and taste like shit," Mark shouts from the kitchen.

Not wanting to make him wait any longer, I rush into his room and turn on the shower. I'm stripped down and about to step inside when I realise I never grabbed any stuff. With Banner in the shower I normally occupy, it's not like I can go and get them. Instead, I use what Mark has, wincing when I pick up his mint shower gel. I hate the smell of mint. It reminds me of the leaves my granddad likes to chew on. It's gross.

What's worse is the second I scrub some onto my skin, it burns, yet feels cold. "Holy fucking Christ. Is there acid in this?" I ask myself, picking the bottle up to read it.

I quickly wash it off, but the cool feeling is still there. I'm grateful Levi doesn't use cheap men's shampoo, choosing to use Dove instead. There is no way I'm going to jump in the shower again tonight to wash my hair just because Mark's shampoo has made it feel like cardboard. I made the mistake of using it when I first got here. It dried rock hard and looked thick with grease.

My mind wanders back to the park and the way Banner held me. He was about to kiss me, there was no mistaking it. And he would have, if that lad hadn't kicked his football at us. We would have picked up where we left off to if Mark hadn't had called me. I can't even be mad at Mark or the lad for interrupting the moment—the perfect moment for a first kiss—because they didn't know about it. And deep down, a small part of me is glad the lad kicked the ball at us. My insecurities are screaming at me that I'll lose him if we ever take our relationship further.

Down on paper, this situation seems pretty straight forward: the girl should just tell the boy she loves him. It's the advice I would give someone if they were in my situation. The only difference is my feelings. I feel deeply for Banner. The kind of love that comes only once in a lifetime. I've loved before, but it's nothing compared to how I feel about Banner. My heart never skipped when they walked into a room, and I never got that rush I get when I'm around Banner. I also never looked at them the way I look at him. I see beyond the tattoos and good looks. I see him. Just him.

I step out of the shower and wrap a towel around my body and one around my hair.

I'm faced with a serious dilemma: I don't have any clothes. I smack my forehead, wondering what to do.

Peeking my head out the bathroom, I find Mark's room still empty and his door still closed. I tip toe over, slowly and quietly pushing down the handle and pulling it open. Voices are coming from the kitchen, one belonging to Mark, the other Levi, which means Banner is still in the shower.

Great. This couldn't get any worse.

Deciding to make a run for it before he finishes in the shower, I open the door and run across the hall to my room. I slam the door closed behind me and walk over to my chest of drawers. Finding a pair of pants, a bra, and some comfy, warm pyjamas, I drop my towel to the floor.

The sound of my door opening has a startled scream escaping me. I bend down to pick up my towel, but it's too late. Banner stands in the doorway, his jaw slack as he looks me over. I quickly cover myself, frozen in place and too stunned to speak.

He just saw me naked.

He clears his throat, his eyes still on my half-naked body. I shift, wanting to hide, yet... feeling exhilarated at the same time. I've never had anyone look at me the way he's looking at me right now.

"I forgot to take some clothes into the bathroom," he croaks out.

When I realise I'm still standing here, clutching the towel to my body without saying anything in return, I die of mortification. I want him to stay as much as I want him to leave.

He takes a step forward, his eyes hooded.

"Are you two gonna stare at each other all day or are you going to get dressed and come eat the dinner I've slaved away cooking?"

Mark's voice is like an ice-cold bucket of water thrown at me. I jump, nearly dropping the towel.

"Y-yeah."

"I was just getting some clothes," Banner rushes out before quickly grabbing his duffel bag from the floor.

He sends me one more intense gaze that holds a promise before leaving the room. I watch the space he just left for a few more moments, but Mark standing in the doorway snaps me out of it.

"Um, can you shut the door, so I can get dressed?"

The grin that spreads across his face has me narrowing my eyes at him.

"I can see why you have the hots for him. Did you see his arse?"

I gape at him before reaching over my bed and grabbing one of my small pillows. I throw it across the room. "Get out!"

He winks, not moving from the doorway. "Come on, did you at least look?"

"Mark!" I warn, feeling my cheeks heat.

"He was totally checking you out. And by the way, you're showing nipple," he whisper-yells.

I scream, grabbing another pillow, at the same time trying to keep the towel around me. "Get out!"

He laughs, shutting the door before the pillow can hit him. "I'm dishing out dinner. Does anyone want some tasty buns with it?" he yells through the door.

"Buns? We don't have any buns," Levi yells back.

"We do," Mark calls back, laughter in his voice.

"With a Sunday dinner, though? It's random."

I don't hear Mark's reply since he's moved away from the door. Probably filling Levi in on what happened.

I take my time getting dressed, not ready to leave the confines of my room. I don't know how I'm going to face Banner after he just saw me naked. Or the fact that I now know he was gawking at my peeping nipples.

I fall face first onto the bed, screaming into the blanket.

I just had to go and make an arse of myself.

Chapter 11

When I wake up the next morning, it's to find Banner staring at me. I jump, shocked at seeing his face so close, even if it is a pretty sight to wake up to.

"Why are you staring at me, you creeper?"

When I notice the serious expression on his face, I bite my bottom lip worriedly. "We need to talk."

"Can it wait until after coffee?" I ask hopefully.

He shoots down my request. "Nope."

"Okay."

We stay lying down, facing each other, my hand tucked under my cheek.

"About yesterday"

Feeling my face redden, I hold my hand up and cut him off. "Please, we don't need to talk about it. It was an accident. You didn't know I was in the room."

He looks away briefly, before facing me. "You couldn't look at me all night."

"You saw me naked," I grumble, embarrassed.

He grins, flashing his teeth. "I did." I smack his arm, causing him to laugh. "Would it help you if you saw me naked?"

My face is probably redder than a tomato. I throw the blanket off me, feeling too hot. "No. It really wouldn't."

He sits up as I get out of bed and grab his hoody to fight off the chill. I don't turn around when I brush my hair, not able to look at him without turning redder.

"What will it take for you to look at me? I miss your blue eyes."

"They're green," I scoff, hurt he doesn't know the colour of my eyes, even if he is half right.

I hear him move, getting more comfortable before he answers. "No, your eyes are blue with flecks of green. There's more blue in them than there is green. You just have to look close enough."

I spin around, trying to gauge whether he's telling me the truth or not. His expression hasn't changed. I glance at the mirror, trying not to look at my eyes. It's hard, and in the end, I do, seeing exactly what he sees. I swallow the knot in my throat.

My nan always said to keep the ones that pay attention and know when you get your hair cut or buy a new pair of shoes. Those were the rare ones.

"What are your plans today?"

"I'm actually going to meet up with the lads to play footy this afternoon. Do you want to come with me?"

As much as I want to watch him run around a football field in a pair of shorts, I have other plans.

"I'm sorry; I can't. I messaged Jordan yesterday to tell her I would meet her today. She'll be here in an hour or so."

"She not pissed at you about Max?"

I laugh, remembering him asking her to call him if she fancied Lake for an hour as we left the café. I was torn between being mortified and amused when Lake started attacking him.

"She's fine. She's used to dealing with it, and she knew he was only joking."

"I don't know. He's a lad."

I glare at him, cocking my hip to the side. "So, if you had a girlfriend and another girl offered to join, you wouldn't mind?"

"If that's your way of asking me if I've had a threesome, then yes, but I was never in a relationship with those girls. Would I do it if I was in a relationship? Fuck no. I'd never let the girl I love be seen or touched by another person—girl or boy."

I rub my chest at his confession of being in a threesome. That is information I'd rather he had lied to me about. And hearing him talk about loving a girl, even one that doesn't exist yet, hurts more than I care to admit.

"I need to shower. I don't want to be late."

"Are you mad at me?" he asks, jumping out of bed. I bite my lip as he walks towards me, his muscles tensing. He's only in a pair of boxers, and they don't hide the package beneath them.

I look away when I'm caught staring, grabbing some jeans and a T-shirt. "No. Why would I be mad? What you do or don't do doesn't concern me."

"It doesn't?" he asks. The bite in his tone has me pausing to face him.

"No. We're just friends, aren't we."

His jaw clenches as he looks away, the veins in his neck bulging. "So, if I went out and got with a girl, you wouldn't care?"

I'd die.

"Why are we talking about this?" I whisper, looking up at him through my lashes.

He runs his fingers through his hair, making it stick up. "I don't know. I just don't want you to be mad at me."

"I'm not mad at you," I tell him truthfully. I'm hurt, not mad.

"Good," he tells me, before stepping forward and pulling me in for a hug.

I hug him back, blinking back tears. I've always played 'what if' when it came to him meeting a girl, and it always made my stomach cramp at the mere thought. I want him. And deep down, he's mine, even if he doesn't know it.

When I pull back, his face is close, his lips a breath away from mine. I blink rapidly, feeling my heart beat against my chest. There's no doubt he can't feel it. I feel my eyes droop when he runs a finger along my jaw.

Two taps on the door startle us apart. "Wake up, Jordan will be here in an hour, Emma," Levi shouts through the door.

"I'm up," I shout back, trying to calm my racing heart.

Banner groans, looking up at the ceiling. "For fucks sake."

"You okay?"

His smile is forced when he looks down at me. "Yeah. I'll let you get ready. I'd better go meet Tom."

"Okay," I tell him shakily, quickly grabbing my underwear before rushing out of the room.

Levi's standing with his arms crossed just outside, startling a small squeak from me. I put my hand to my chest.

"What are you doing standing there?"

"Did I interrupt something? You two sounded out of breath."

I roll my eyes. "No. We were talking about something. And stop acting like my dad."

"I know you love him. I know he loves you, too. What I can't figure out is if you two know it."

"I wish people would stop saying that. What if you're wrong and I make a fool out of myself?"

He scoffs. "Honey, I'm gay, not stupid. You couldn't cut the sexual tension between you two, it's that thick. Just make a move, put the poor sod out of his misery."

"I'll think about it," I tell him, shutting the bathroom door behind me before he can say anything else.

Banner is gone by the time I leave the bathroom. I sigh, stepping into my room before Jordan gets here.

My gaze flicks to the bed when I see it's made. I smile as I walk over, finding one of my flowers laying on top of a note.

Emma,

Please don't be mad at me. I know what I said upset you, but I don't want there to be secrets between us. You've confided in me with so much. I would hate for you to find out down the line when we're married with kids, and have you hating me for not telling you. And you asked me. I couldn't lie to you.

I will bring you Indian for dinner, so don't eat.

Forgive me.

Banner.

I read the letter three times before I realise a few tears have fallen and I'm smiling. I can't tell whether he's joking about the marriage and children, but I can't hide the effect those words have on me.

I quickly grab my phone from the bedside table and type out a text to him.

ME: I'll always forgive you.

It takes a few minutes for him to reply, but when he does, I smile.

BANNER: What are we calling the kids?

ME: LOL

BANNER: I reckon we should have 4. 2 girls and 2 boys.

ME: Next you'll be telling me we'll have dog, a tree house, and a big wedding.

BANNER: Nope to the big wedding. You'd hate that. We're going to have a small one. Just our close friends and family: Lake and her boyfriend, your grandparents, Mark and Levi, and my mum, dad and siblings. Yes, to the dog. We can call it Bruno. The tree house may take time, but we'll do it.

ME: Are you for real? LOL. You do make me laugh.

BANNER: You'll see. Speak to you later. Tom's here.

BANNER: And while I'm gone, try to think on what we can call our second daughter. I'm at a loss.

I'm smiling when I roll my eyes, my stomach giddy with excitement. But I need to know

ME: What's our first daughter's name?

BANNER: Easy. Lara Catherine Banner.

I flop down on the edge of my bed, feeling tears fall and drop down to my lap. He sounds so serious. If he's not, then this is a cruel joke playing with me like this.

I don't message him back, too afraid of what I'll say—and what he'll say in return.

Knocking on the front door reminds me of Jordan. I rush out of the room, waving at Levi when he goes to get up from the sofa.

"I'll get it."

I open the door to find Jordan standing next to another girl. She's tiny. She's also really beautiful. But something about her seems broken. It's her eyes, I realise, the emptiness inside them, the lack of life. I should know; I looked at the same dead expression staring back at me in the mirror for years.

She looks to her feet when she notices me staring, and I instantly feel bad. I never liked people analysing me—still don't—and I can see she feels the same.

"Hey, this is my friend, Rosie. We thought we could hang out together today, if that's okay?"

"That's fine. Did you want to hang out here or go somewhere?"

She looks to Rosie, who bites her bottom lip. "I don't mind."

"It's raining, and I just had my hair dyed. Would you mind if we stayed here?"

I nod, opening the door for them to step inside. Levi gets up from the sofa when he sees we've got guests, but falters when he looks at Rosie.

My gaze moves away from him when I hear a whimper. I turn to find Rosie shaking, and watch as she moves half a step behind Jordan, like she's seeking protection.

Jordan gives us an apologetic look. "I'm sorry. I didn't realise you had company. We can go grab coffee."

"No, it's fine. I'm going to surprise my boyfriend at work. You guys stay in the warmth. Is that okay?" Levi asks softly, his eyes on Rosie. Her cheeks turn pink, but she gives a barely perceptible nod, her eyes downcast.

"You sure?" I ask, hating that he feels like he has to leave, but at the same time loving him for his consideration towards a stranger.

"Yeah. I was going to go later anyway, so it's no problem."

He grabs his keys and jacket, walking towards us slowly. Rosie steps out of his way, and as he reaches us, Jordan clears her throat. "Thank you," she says quietly.

"It's fine. You three stay out of trouble," he tells us, before leaving.

When the door shuts, Rosie visibly relaxes, her face ashen. "I'm so sorry."

Jordan wraps an arm around her. "It's okay. You didn't run off, so it's a start."

I'm missing something vital here.

"I think it was his size and all those tattoos."

"Rosie was one of the victims from last year. She still has trouble being around males," Jordan explains.

Rosie looks up at me, sorrow in her eyes. "I'm sorry. We came here and basically kicked him out. I just couldn't form any words."

"He's a softie. He might have all those tattoos, but he wouldn't hurt a fly. We tried to get him to stomp on a spider last week, and instead he caught it in a jar and set it free."

She smiles, her face lightening. "At least he didn't run screaming."

I laugh. "No, but me and Mark did. It was huge," I tell her, holding my hands together to show her. "Would you like a drink?"

"Coffee," they both say, then start laughing.

"I hear you. I've not had a cup yet."

"You poor thing," Jordan says.

She gets it. Banner would just roll his eyes at me and tell me to wait. He's not really a big coffee or drinker—or tea. It's weird.

I head into the kitchen, flicking the kettle on and grabbing cups out of the cupboard.

"How was your visit with your friends?" Jordan asks as they both follow behind.

"Great. I really miss her, more now she's here to talk to. Before, I thought she was gone forever."

"What do you mean?"

I finish making their coffee and step into the front room, taking a seat in the love chair. Since they shared about Rosie, it's the least I can do to share some of my past. I normally avoid any topic of my past, hating the empty feeling I get inside my chest.

"When we were at high school, she was involved in an accident with her mum and brother. She thought she was the reason her brother had died. She ran away because she couldn't bear to face her parents. She was out of her mind with grief and self-hate. The accident wasn't anyone's fault, though. A year ago, her boyfriend found her parents. She had been homeless, so his nan had taken her in. When Max found out about her past, he contacted her parents. She was shocked when she found them downstairs, her brother alive."

"Oh, my god, that sounds horrible. I bet she's just as happy as you about being back in each other's lives."

I shrug, then take a chance when I tell them a bit more. "I was going through something when she ran away. I suffered with depression and missed her like crazy. But I was also mad at her for leaving me when I needed her the most. When I found out she was alive and back in our home town, it helped me move forward. I just don't like the thought of losing her again."

"I'm sure she wouldn't let that happen."

"Yeah."

Clearing her throat, Rosie sits forward. "Jordan said you're volunteering to help with the cake sale. Do you want any help?"

"If you want to help, more the merrier, but I'm good if you can't," I tell her, not wanting to push her. I can see she's in a bad place still, but she's also a fighter. I can see it in her eyes, no matter how blank her gaze gets when she's lost in thought.

"I want to. I love decorating cakes."

I brighten. "Are you good at it?"

"Yep."

"Great! I'm only good at the basics. Anything beyond plopping icing on the cake is a no go. If I bake them, do you want to come and decorate them?"

"I'd like that. Are you going to cook one to donate for the raffle? I can help decorate that, too, if you'd like. Most of it I can do at home until the cake is baked."

"That sounds awesome. When I was asked, I said yes, not thinking about that part of the baking," I tell her, laughing. I'm also glad for the change in subject, no longer wanting to live in the past.

By the time we finish planning what we're going to do, it's late in the evening and time for them to go. I walk them outside.

"It was lovely meeting you, Rosie."

"Same. I don't go out much, but if you ever want to hang out at mine, or meet up somewhere quiet, call me. I'll get Jordan to text you my number."

Jordan looks proud as she listens to Rosie. It's just a guess, but I'm presuming this is a big step for her.

"I will. Thank you. And the quieter the better; I hate crowds."

She blushes, ducking her head. "Me too."

I smile at her, finding her adorable, before turning to Jordan. "Thanks for coming on such short notice. I just have a busy couple of weeks and didn't want to keep you waiting."

"It's fine. We were only going to sit in and watch movies, and we can do that when we get back. Thank you for having us, and tell Levi I said thank you, too."

"And that I promise to try and relax the next time I see him," Rosie adds.

"Don't push yourself. Just do what you feel is comfortable. But I do promise you neither Levi, Mark, nor Banner would ever hurt you. Mark and Banner are bigger built than Levi, and have more tattoos, but they'd sooner cut off their arm than hurt a girl."

"Thank you," she whispers, and something passes between us. Sometimes when she looks at me, I wonder if she knows we've been through something similar, except hers was much worse and a lot more horrific.

I wave them off, and just as I'm about to turn inside, a chill runs down my spine. I look around the darkening street, seeing no one that stands out, but the hairs on the back of my neck stand on end, telling me otherwise.

I quickly close the door, grateful the residents of the building need a key fob to get inside. I rush up the stairs, to the first floor, and into our flat, slamming the door shut behind me.

The feeling still doesn't go away, so I head to my bedroom, where I can spend the rest of the evening tucked up in bed waiting for Banner to get back.

Something isn't right here in Whithall. There's been a series of rapes, and now women are getting murdered. It's frightening to know something so heinous, so tragic, could happen so close to home. It breaks my heart knowing families are losing loved ones.

However, the sick feeling I get in my stomach when I feel someone watching me, is different, like I know who the person watching me is.

A sense of foreboding creeps up my spine, screaming at me that I won't like what's to come.

That I'm once again trapped inside my own prison, only almost free.

Chapter 12

Wednesday comes around quickly, and before I know it, I'm leaving the house to go and meet Becky. We're going to meet at the university and walk over to the all-night café close by.

It snowed the night before, leaving a dust of flakes on the ground. I pull my scarf up higher when the cold night air hits my cheeks.

I should have stayed at home. It's freezing.

The walk isn't far, but I'm regretting not taking up Banner's offer to drive me. I would have said yes but I didn't want him out on the roads, not in this weather.

A snowflake twirls through the air in front of me, promising more to come. We may have four seasons, but we never have them in the months we're supposed to. It's going to be spring soon and instead of sun and flowers springing from the ground, all we have is rain or snow.

I'm nearing the pathway that leads to the English building when I feel eyes watching me from outside my field of vision. I scan the darkened path subtly, not seeing anything. But that doesn't mean someone isn't there. I can feel their eyes on me, sizing me up.

Being thoroughly aware that girls are being found murdered, and knowing Darren is out there, walking free, has only fed my paranoia. I feel like I'm constantly looking over my shoulder, expecting an attack to happen at any moment.

Footsteps creeping behind me, crunching in the snow, have me moving at a faster pace. The pathways have been gritted, so whoever it is must be walking in the grass, hiding behind the bushes.

My heart begins to race, my breath puffing out like a cloud of smoke in front of me as I begin to jog, my stomach twisting in knots.

Just as I'm about to enter the courtyard outside our building, a dark figure kicks off the wall. I come to a sudden stop, nearly tripping over my own feet when I see who is standing right in front of me. I feel the blood drain from my face, bile rising in my throat at the sight of my nightmare.

Darren looks different, nothing like the skinny, pale kid I remember him being. He's put on weight and muscle, looking healthier than I've ever seen him. No longer does he have red eyes with dark circles under them. His skin even has colour.

"Emma."

I take a step back, my hand going into my pocket to get my phone. If I thought I wouldn't collapse after a few steps, I would run home. As it is, I don't want to risk him finding out where I live or have him near me when I'm vulnerable.

"What are you doing here?" I ask shakily, holding one for Banner's speed dial.

"Please don't—I just want to talk," he says, taking a step closer, his hands up.

I take a step back, putting the phone in my pocket when I see the call has connected.

"I don't have anything to say to you. I want you to leave." I move further away, feeling my entire body tremble—and not from the cold.

He pauses before taking a few steps back, his face pale. "I'm not going to hurt you. I promise. I just want to talk."

"Are you following me?" I blurt out, glancing over my shoulder briefly before turning back to him. I no longer feel any eyes on me, but some primal part of me is worried it wasn't Darren I felt watching me. I don't think Darren being in front of me is a coincidence.

He looks taken aback. "No. Why? I promise, I just want to talk. You didn't reply to my letter."

"I don't want to talk to you," I tell him, before deciding to leave. If I know Banner, he will drive over here, so I head to the carpark, wanting to get away from him.

"Please, Emma. I'm sorry. I'm so fucking sorry for what I did to you."

I stop and spin around to face him, nearly causing him to bump into me. Memories from my attack assault me, and I feel the fear I felt that night. It hits me so hard I struggle for breath. Darren watches me as I bring myself back to reality, and wisely takes a step back.

"Sorry for what you did to me? What about my sister—are you sorry for killing her?"

He glances away, having the audacity to look ashamed. "I didn't kill Lara. I gave her the drugs, yes, but they weren't mine. I had sold out and she begged me"

I hold my hand up. "Stop! I don't want to hear it. Leave me alone and stop following me, otherwise I'm going to the police."

"I just want you to hear me out. I need to explain, Emma."

I grit my teeth. "No! I don't owe you anything, Darren. I don't have to listen to a word you have to say, and I won't."

Tyres squeal in the car park, and I know it's Banner without looking. He's not even next to me but already I feel safer.

"I owe you everything."

"Get the fuck away from her!" Banner yells as he comes storming up behind us. He doesn't stop when he reaches us.

"I just wanted to—Fuck!" Darren holds his bleeding nose as he falls to the floor. I gasp, before rushing over to Banner and pulling him back.

"Stop! I don't want you getting into trouble."

Banner doesn't look at me as he glares down at Darren. "Stay the fuck away from her, Darren. You've put her through enough."

"I need to tell her something. Please. I'll only take five minutes."

I have to look away from his pleading face, almost feeling sorry for him. He's not the Darren I remember. Back when we were younger, he would never apologise. He was cocky, arrogant and sure of himself. I never liked him, but I put up with him for Lake. I never understood what she saw in him. She was my best friend, though, and I'd do anything for her. Even put up with a low life like Darren.

"I don't give a fuck if it takes two. You aren't talking to her."

He looks to me, his eyes pleading. "Did you read the letter?"

"No, I didn't."

"Read it, please."

I watch him get up before answering. "I destroyed it. Darren, go home. I don't want to see you or speak to you."

He nods like he understands. "If you change your mind, contact your lawyer. I gave them my details, explaining I wanted to talk to you."

"Go, before I deck you again. You've got no fucking right coming here and doing this to her," Banner growls.

"I know. I'm sorry. I'm just sorry," he says, sounding broken.

I thought seeing him drowning in guilt, broken up over his sins, would make me happy, but it doesn't. I just feel confused. I've hated him for so long. I hated him so much it ate away at me. I would daydream over what I would say to him, what I would do differently —what I would do to him. In none of my imaginary scenarios did I feel sorry for him.

Not able to look at him any longer, I pull harder on Banner's arm. "Come on, I want to go. I'll email my teachers and say I'm sick."

Banner doesn't say a word as we turn back to his car. Taking a glance over my shoulder, I'm surprised to see Darren still standing there, holding his nose. He looks defeated. Something catches his attention, because his head snaps to the side like he's seen something.

A shiver runs up my spine at the look he gives me, like he wants to call out my name.

"Did he hurt you?" Banner asks as he pulls open his door. He had been in such a rush he left the car running.

I get in the car, rubbing my hands together. "No." I let him walk around the car and get in before speaking. "Thank you for coming for me. I didn't know what to do. And I didn't want him following me home."

Instead of driving me home straight away, he faces me, reaching over and pulling me in for a hug. "When I heard his voice over the phone, I thought my heart had stopped beating. I kept picturing the worst. Are you sure you're okay? He didn't do anything?"

We pull apart, and I force a smile to reassure him. I don't think Darren would have hurt me tonight, however, my judgement has been impaired before when it comes to him. There's no telling what he would do.

"I promise he didn't do anything. Can we go home? I don't think I can stomach meeting Becky or going to class right now. I just want to go home."

He nods, putting the car into gear. I take my phone out, explaining to Becky I'm heading back home because I'm not feeling well.

Banner takes my hand, holding it in his lap as he drives, only letting go when he needs to change gears.

When we get back home, exhaustion hits me. I ache everywhere. We're just walking up the stairs to the flat when I hear Mark and Levi's hurried voices.

"He's not answering, Levi. If something's happened to her"

"Hey, it's okay. She'll be okay. I'm sure she just forgot her books or something," Levi answers, trying to soothe him.

I give Banner a questioning look and he grimaces. "I kind of ran out before I could explain anything. But they knew it was you calling, 'cause I told them you'd probably forgotten something and was calling me to drop it off to you."

"Banner? Is that you?" Mark yells, rushing to the top of the stairs. When he sees me with him, his face turns pale and he walks down the few steps to get to me. "Thank fuck. Are you okay? Did something happen?" He pulls away to glare at Banner. "The next time something happens, don't fucking rush off. You're lucky I don't lay you out for scaring the shit out of me."

"Sorry, mate. I heard Darren's voice over the phone and just panicked. I didn't stop and think. I'm sorry."

Mark's eyes widen. "Darren? Are you okay? Did he hurt you?"

I slap his arms away from inspecting for injuries. "I'm fine. He didn't touch me."

"What the fuck *did he* want?"

"He wanted to explain—to say sorry." I shrug, trying to erase the picture of his expression when I told him no. I hate myself for feeling sorry for him. He ruined my life. I could have gone off to college with my other friends had he not destroyed what remaining part of my soul I had left. The pieces I had, he scattered. And now I'm standing here feeling sorry for him. It's not right.

Mark's face is filled with anger when he looks to Levi. "You fucking hearing this? He's sorry. Fucking sorry. Like that is going to make up for the shit he caused."

"Let's get inside. My balls are blue, they are that cold," Levi says, pushing Mark towards the door.

"Where were you two going? I thought you were staying in tonight," I remind them, looking around the room. Before I left, they had the X-Box out and was playing Call of Duty.

Mark glares at Banner one more time. "To look for you two. When he didn't answer his phone or come back right away, we decided to come find you ourselves."

I give him a sweet smile. "Thank you. But I'm okay, I swear."

"Should we call the police?"

"Yes," Banner snaps as I say, "No."

"What do you mean, no?" he demands, watching me take my coat off.

I don't look at him when I answer, dropping into the love seat and curling up. "Because he didn't do anything. I don't want to waste police time on nothing. It will only get my hopes up for a restraining order, only for them to say they won't issue one without cause."

"He beat you the fuck up," Banner growls. "That's cause enough."

"He's right. Darren shouldn't be following you around, Emma," he tells me, before facing Banner. "Please tell me you knocked the fucker out for me. If I ever lay eyes on him, I'm gonna kill him."

"Babe, calm down. Emma doesn't need to hear this," Levi says smoothly, coaxing him away from the door like he's afraid Mark will escape and do what he promised. Kill Darren.

"Guys, please," I beg.

"I laid one on him, yeah. He's lucky that's all I did. I think we should still mention it to your lawyer. If something happens, we might need to have this on file."

"Please, Banner, can we just drop it. I'm cold, hungry, and just want you guys around me."

His expression softens as he joins me on the sofa. His cold body warms up to mine. The loon didn't even bother pulling on a coat when he raced out of here to find me. I want to reprimand him for being careless, but what he did was also incredibly sweet.

"Okay. Mark was gonna cook chicken fajitas, so why don't we eat that, kick some arse on Call of Duty, then watch a movie in bed?"

"Sounds like a plan," I tell him, forcing a smile. "And thank you. I don't know what I would do without you."

"You're never going to have to find out," he whispers.

Chapter 13

The café Milly asked me to join her at is dead when I meet her on Friday evening. The place is completely deserted. Scanning the room, I find her sitting in a booth at the back, facing the door. Which is something I always do.

When she notices me walking towards her, a smile lights up her beautiful face. She stands to greet me, moving out of the booth.

"Emma. It's lovely to meet you in person," she says. "Here, you take a seat while I order us some drinks. What would you like?"

Since I'm too nervous, I opt not to have coffee. "Can I have a hot chocolate, please?"

"Of course. Won't be a second," she says, before walking elegantly over to the counter.

While she's busy ordering, I take the time to look her over. She looks younger than she did when we booked our appointment over Skype. She's not dressed like my old therapist, either. Instead of a suit, she's dressed in jeans and a woolly jumper. It makes me feel at ease. It's also refreshing not to be in an office, enclosed within four walls. I don't feel like I'm in a prison here; I can leave at any time.

I don't know what today will entail, whether she wants me to fill her in on more of what happened to me or not, or if this is just an introduction.

Even though there is no one here but the waitress and a cook, I still don't feel comfortable talking so openly about what happened to me.

Milly walks back over, sitting the steaming cup of hot chocolate down in front of me. "Here you go, lovely."

I fidget in my seat, unsure of what to do or say. I finally decide to wait for her to lead, and then see what happens from there.

"First of all, I want you to know you don't have to talk to me about anything you don't want to. I won't push you into something you aren't ready for either. Don't think of me as a therapist while you're with me. You can talk to me like I'm your friend, but know, whatever is shared between the both of us, will go no further. Are you okay with that?"

"I am."

"Super. I like to get that part out of the way, otherwise we might just sit here and stare into our cups. And although that would be fine with me, you are coming to me for a reason."

I love her bluntness, it's refreshing. She keeps her voice soft, making me feel at ease.

"How are you finding it here in Whithall?" she asks, taking a sip of her drink, like we're old friends.

"I like living with my cousin, Mark, and his boyfriend, Levi. I also have a friend named Banner. He's showed me around some, but mostly to restaurants to try out his favourite foods."

She giggles, and I relax in my seat. "Sounds like my kind of friend. Where has he taken you that you've liked the best?"

I don't even have to think about it. Our time spent with Lake and Max had been my favourite place. "Fun 'N Cups. My friends came to visit me from out of town and we went there. The food was great, but I think I preferred the company more."

"What do you mean?"

I look around the empty room, chewing my bottom lip. "Even though this place is empty, I still feel kind of tense. When we were at Fun 'N Cups, I got so lost in the three of them that I forgot where I even was. It was nice and relaxing."

"Sounds like you had a good time," she says softly, smiling.

"I did."

"I'm glad."

I look away from the window to face the woman in front of me, needing to ask her the one question I've been dying to have answered. The guilt has been eating away at me all week. I can't talk about this with the men in my life, they wouldn't understand. Milly is Switzerland.

"Can I ask you something?"

"You can ask me anything, Emma."

"Do you think something is wrong with me for feeling sorry for the person who attacked me?"

Her expression doesn't change as she drops her cup to the table. "I don't think anything is wrong with you at all. It just proves what a compassionate young lady you are." She pauses, watching me intently. "Did something happen? When we booked the meeting, I was under the impression your attacker was in prison."

"I saw him the other week. At first, I thought I imagined it, but after my cousin looked into it, we found out the same day he had been out for a while. And then, on Wednesday, he was outside of the English building, waiting for me to arrive."

"Did he hurt you?" she asks quickly, her relaxed, soft expression turning serious, concerned.

"No. He wanted to talk, to apologise, but I called Banner and he came and got me. But… for those fifteen minutes, I didn't just see my attacker. I saw someone else, someone broken. I felt sorry for him."

"You're a remarkable woman, Emma. I'm not saying what you're feeling is part of the road to forgiveness. People find that in their own way. Nobody is saying you have to forgive your attacker, and in most cases, people don't. I've counselled women who have known their attacker or abuser, found a way to forgive them, and said it helped them move on. Not all incidents are the same though, Emma."

"I don't know why I feel this way," I tell her, rubbing my chest.

"Did he apologise?"

I shrug. "He tried to, but I cut him off. He took everything from me. He might not have forced those drugs down my sister's throat, but he sold them to her. He knew she was in love with him, too, and he messed her around."

"And then he attacked you?" she states matter-of-factly.

I nod, staring back outside the window, watching snowflakes float down under the streetlights. "I want to hate him. I *do* hate him. But I'm so confused, too. A part of me wanted to hear what he had to say, but the other was scared of what he wanted to tell me. I feel like I'm finally moving on with my life. What if he says something I don't want to hear, and I go back to that dark place?"

"You've had a traumatic experience. You lost your sister, you were brutally attacked, and from the notes your therapist sent over, you had to deal with unloving parents. It couldn't have been easy for you. You've already taken that first step to moving on. You should be proud of yourself, Emma."

"It's not really an accomplishment," I state dryly, feeling defensive all of a sudden over her praise.

She lets it sweep over her head. "I disagree. I'd say it's one of the biggest you could make. You've felt that loneliness, that empty feeling in the pit of your stomach, and the desire to end everything just so you can get five minutes of peace. You've wanted to keep your mind silent from the constant nightmares running through them. To get from that dark place, to the one you are in right now, I'd say it's a hell of an accomplishment. Don't put yourself down."

My cheeks heat at her scolding. She's also spot on with her words about the silence. It's why I tried to overdose after my sister had died and I was attacked. I just wanted it all to end.

I had risen from the sink to find my reflection staring back at me. I didn't like what I saw; it scared me. Once I realised what I had done, I stuck my fingers down my throat and vomited all the tablets I had taken.

"I just don't know what to do. Should I hear him out or just ignore the fact I ever saw him?"

She gives me a sad smile. "Only you can answer that, lovely. But you don't have to decide straight away. Have you spoken to your friend and family about this?"

I shake my head, fiddling with the handle on my cup. "I don't think they'll understand. They hate him as much as I do for what he did to me."

"Because they love you," she states softly. "What he has to say won't change what happened in the past. He would still be involved in the events leading up to your sister's death, and responsible for your attack. What you need to decide is whether whatever he has to say will ease your mind or answer any unspoken questions. And you don't even need to meet him alone. You could hire a mediator to witness the exchange. And I'm sure your cousin, his boyfriend, or your friend would go with you. But if you don't feel comfortable with either, I'd be more than happy to come with you."

"Can I think about it?"

Her eyes soften. "Emma, you can have all the time in the world. You don't have to find all the answers today."

"Thank you."

"My pleasure." She smiles. "Now, I know you have class in twenty minutes, so we should get moving. Did you drive, or would you like me to drop you off? Since it's snowing, it might take us a while to get there."

"Banner dropped me off here. He's waiting outside to take me. Thank you for offering though."

"Would you like to set up another meeting now, or wait? I don't want to pressure you into anything. I know my style is unorthodox, but I find more women relax in a familiar setting."

I give her a warm smile. "I will message you a day when I'm free. And I can see why. Surprisingly, this wasn't as bad I thought it would be. I think I opened up more to you than I have to anyone other than Banner."

"I'm glad. That's what I love to hear," she tells me softly. "Be safe, keep warm, and if you need anything, you have my numbers. Don't be afraid to call, day or night. I'm looking forward to our next meeting."

"Me too," I tell her as we head towards the door. When we get outside, I pull my coat tighter around me. "Goodbye, Milly."

"Goodbye, Emma."

I feel her watching me as I get into the car. It isn't until I'm in and the door is shut that she crosses the road to her own car.

"How was it?" Banner asks, pulling slowly out into the slick roads.

"Better than I imagined. She's really nice," I tell him.

"I'm glad. Did you tell her about Darren?"

"Not in detail," I whisper, not wanting to talk about it with him. I know he's mad I won't go to the police. He doesn't understand what it was like answering all those questions after Darren attacked me.

"I'm going to pick you up after class. I'll meet you by the entrance, so don't wander off. That okay?"

"You don't have to do that."

He finishes pulling into a parking space before shutting the car off and facing me. "I want to." He drops his head, licking his lips. "And… if you're not too tired after class, I was wondering if we could talk about something."

I glance at the time on the dashboard. "I still have ten minutes if you want to talk now. Is everything okay?"

He rubs the back of his neck. I sit up straighter, not sure whether I like the look on his face. He's never anxious.

His mouth opens to answer me, when a tap on my window startles me. I scream, flinging myself at Banner and away from the intruder.

I glare when I see Becky standing by the door, her face near enough pressed against the window.

"Come on, let's go inside. Even polar bears would freeze their tits off in this weather."

Banner's hard body shakes beneath me. I groan, lifting myself off him, and wince when the handbrake digs into my hip.

"Did you want me to tell her to wait?" I ask Banner when I've straightened myself out.

He shakes his head, sucking his bottom lip into his mouth to keep from laughing.

"I'm not waiting out here. My nipples are gonna freeze off."

"Go. We wouldn't want her nipples to fall off," he tells me, looking away when he starts to chuckle.

"Hey, I'll have you know, Bess and Tess are good peeps. There's no need to get sarky," she yells through the window.

At that, I have to bite back my own laughter, especially when the few lads that are in our class walk by, trying to look around her to see her chest.

"You named your boobs?" I ask in disbelief when I open the car door.

She looks at me like I've lost my mind. "Don't you?"

"Yeah, do you?" Banner pipes in.

I smack him lightly on the arm and give him a warning look before turning back to Becky. "No, I don't."

When she looks at me with pity, I want to ask her what I've done wrong. Instead, I stay quiet, feeling that would be the wise thing to do.

"My mum's boobs were called Lennie and Rennie. Rennie always pissed her off because it was a little bit bigger than Lennie."

"Are you serious?"

"As a heart attack."

"I've never got that saying," I mutter, ignoring Banner's high-pitched laughter.

"It's fine, Becky, we'll name Emma's, Foxy and Roxy."

Becky bends down to see into the car. "Dude, you can't go naming some chick's tits. Uncool. You wouldn't like us naming your balls."

He chokes on his laughter and starts banging his chest as he coughs through it. I laugh with him, even though I know I'm going to get shit for this later.

"Banner, pull yourself together. I'll wait for you by the doors. They have the front entrance open again."

He's still laughing as I step out of the car, the cold wind whipping my hair around my face.

"Wait, Emma."

With one hand on the roof of the car, I bend down to answer him. "Yeah?"

"You can name my balls any day." He winks, looking sexy as hell, and I blush. It's bad enough he's talking about his balls, let alone winking at me while he's doing so.

I shake my head at him. "Ah, we can call them Itty and Bitty."

His laughter comes to a sudden stop, a horrified expression on his face. "My balls aren't itty or bitty!" I wink at him before pulling back, slamming the door shut behind me, muffling his voice. "They're more like rocky and stocky."

Becky and I start making our way down the path to the English building. "Rocky and Stocky are good names," she says with a straight face. When she sees my wide-eyed expression, she bursts out laughing.

"Can we change the subject?" I mutter dryly.

"Yeah," she answers, sorting herself out. Once she stops laughing, she continues, her voice serious now. "What are we going to do about Mr. Flint?"

Ah, crap!

"I'm glad you mentioned him. I think we should record our classes with him. How much battery do you have?"

We both pull out our phones, and I wince when I see hers. "Not much. I forgot to charge it before I came out. What about you?"

"I've got full battery, but I'm more concerned about my storage. I haven't had chance to get a memory card. I only thought about it this morning."

"If you can, try to keep your phone hidden on your lap. When you see him walking towards you, just hit record. That way you aren't recording the whole two hours."

"I'll do that."

"Come on, let's get this over with," she says, linking her arm through mine.

Chapter 14

Friday's class with Mr. Flint was a bust, but I'm hoping tonight's class won't be. He didn't come near me the entire lesson, but that only served to make me even warier of him—to still be on alert in his lessons. Which is why when Banner offered to take me around town on Monday, I said yes, and grabbed a new memory card for my phone. There was no way I was going to run out of storage now.

It was time for me to head to class soon. I just had to meet up with Becky first. The night was clear, no sign of snow or rain in sight. It was nice to have the break from the freezing temperatures. It was still cold, just not as cold as it had been. Which is why I'm looking for my scarf.

"Hey, Mark, have you seen my pink scarf?" I ask, stepping out of my bedroom.

"No. You had it on when you left with Banner this morning, though. Maybe you left it with him."

"Maybe," I murmur absently. "Thank you."

I step back in my room and walk over to my bedside table, picking my phone up and dialling Banner. I listen to the ring, moving towards the window and pulling the curtain back.

"Hey, beautiful. Miss me already?"

I giggle at his greeting. "Yep."

"You okay?" I hear him moving, and things shuffling in the background.

"Yeah. I was just wondering if I left my pink scarf in your car. I've got to go to class soon. I promised Becky I'd meet up with her to grab a coffee and don't fancy freezing my arse off."

"I don't know, but I'll check. Did you want me to pick you up and take you?" he asks, pausing. "Wait, wasn't Mark meant to be taking you tonight?"

I sigh, watching a car go past, illuminating something in the alley across the street. I stand up straighter, dropping the curtain until only a small gap is left. I don't see anything, and I begin to think my eyes are playing tricks on me.

The situation with Darren, and having the killer on the loose, has got me suffering with paranoia. I'm not the only one, though. Everyone around town seems to be on edge.

"You there?"

"Sorry, um… Yeah, he said he would, but there's no point. It's only a five-minute walk and some chick at work dropped a weight on his foot. I don't really want him out on it."

"I'll be there in five."

"Wait!"

"What?"

"You're hanging with your friends tonight. I don't want you to leave them for me. I'll be fine. I'll keep my phone in hand."

His friends will end up hating me if he keeps blowing them off to spend time with me, and although I'm not ready to be around boisterous men, I don't want him to give that part of his life up.

"Em, I'll be five minutes. I'd rather be spending the night with you than these losers, anyway. Plus, Tom has spent the past few hours texting some chick. I'm bored out of my mind."

I laugh. "Are you sure?"

"I'm sure," he tells me softly. "I'll make sure Becky is there with you before I go anywhere. And I'll be there to pick you up after class as scheduled."

I know he's still worried about Darren cornering me, but I think his overprotective behaviour has to do with another girl showing up murdered. It's all over the news, setting everyone in Whithall on edge.

"Okay. Thank you. I'll make it up to you all. I'll buy you and your friends a crate of beer."

"Don't you dare. If your gonna buy anyone beer, then it will be me. These fuckers don't deserve them."

"Yeah, we do," I hear shouted in the background.

I laugh. "It's rude not to share."

"They don't fucking share with me," he tells me, his voice high.

"He's lying," is shouted.

"Ignore him. He's still learning to tie his shoelaces," he tells me, before shuffling is all I hear. "Dickhead, I'm on the phone." More shuffling. "Em, you still there?"

I hide my amusement when I answer. "Yeah."

"I'll be there in five. I'm leaving now."

"All right. I'll see you in a bit."

"See you soon."

∼

Banner and I got stuck in traffic for fifteen minutes due to a water pipe bursting, so I was late to meet up with Becky.

We didn't have time to go over what we would do if Mr. Flint said something during class, as we were already running behind by a few minutes.

Out of breath, we rush down the hall to our classroom. We slow down to a stop when we reach the door.

Everyone is just taking their seats when I look inside, and I begin to relax, glad they haven't started.

"Speak to you after class," Becky tells me, quickly taking a seat at her table.

I walk to the back of the class, pulling my books out on the way.

"Hey, Emma."

I look down at one of the lads in the class, shocked he knows my name. "Um, hi."

"How's your day going?"

I look to the back of the room where my table is, desperate to sit down before Mr. Flint sees me. "Good, thanks," I tell him, stepping away.

He glances at me, up and down, making me recoil. "Did you do anything special?"

I pause, not wanting to be rude and ignore him. "N—"

"Emma! Is there a reason you are holding my class up?"

The lad speaking to me winces, but instead of explaining he was detaining me, he turns to the front of the class, acting like he can't see me.

"No. I'm sorry," I mumble, but loud enough so he can hear me. I quickly take a seat.

"Sorry? People here want to learn. I won't tolerate your behaviour. If you can't make it to class on time, then don't come. And before you or anyone else get any ideas, this isn't a place to pick up boys," Mr. Flint snaps.

My face burns with embarrassment. "I'm sorry. It won't happen again," I tell him, not wanting to argue with him. Everyone's attention is on me, and it takes a lot for me not to run out crying. I hate being centre of attention.

"See that it doesn't. And you can stay behind Friday after class."

"But I—" The sharp look he gives me has my mouth snapping shut and shrinking back into my seat.

There is no way I can be alone with him. Not a chance in hell.

"Not another word. I have a class to teach," he hisses.

My mouth drops open in shock, my gaze turning to Becky. She's turned a little in her seat, so she's half facing me.

"What the fuck?" she mouths.

I shrug, mouthing back, "I don't know."

We both turn back to the front, not wanting to give him any more ammunition to yell at us.

All through class I'm tense, waiting for him to come to me. Even as we near the end of the lesson, my anxiousness doesn't let up, every muscle in my body aching.

The clock reads nine-fifteen. I have five minutes left. I'm too busy staring at the clock to notice Mr. Flint step behind me. He must have gone around the side of the classroom, sneaking up on me, because he sure as hell didn't come down the aisle I'm next to.

I feel his hands grip the back of my chair, his knuckles touching me, and I freeze, my back ramrod straight. Remembering what Becky said to do, I slowly slide my phone out from between my legs and place it onto my lap. Picturing the buttons I memorised, I press record. I just hope it works, since I didn't have chance to prepare.

His breath hits my cheek when he bends down to talk to me. "Don't even think about missing Friday's lesson. The consequences will be greater than you can imagine if you do. You'll take your punishment, Emma," he bites out, his lips brushing across my cheek. I move away, ready to give him what for. I'm not about to let another male intimidate me.

Before I have a chance to speak, he steps away, walking down the aisle to the front of the class. He stops next to Becky's chair, looking down at her. I can't see his expression from here, but whatever it is, it has Becky turning quickly in her chair.

As soon as it's time to leave, I pack up my books, rushing down the aisle before anyone else can stop me. I take Becky's hand, not even stopping to check she has everything with her.

I only slow down once I know we're away from the classroom, slowing down to talk to her. "Did you see him?"

She looks over her shoulder briefly to check if anyone is listening. "What were you daydreaming about?" she snaps. "I was trying to get your attention for five minutes to warn you he was sneaking up on you."

"You saw him?"

She gives me an 'are you kidding me' look. "Um, yeah. He was watching you the whole time, too. He walked along the side wall and then along the back wall until he was standing behind you. You need to stay alert, Emma. Did you at least record it?"

I ignore her reprimand, already knowing how stupid I was. "Let me check it worked." I pull out my phone, frowning when I see it's not recording. I go through my menu, clicking on videos, and growl. Then it dawns on me. I didn't have it set up to be on record because we were late coming in. "Shit! I forgot to set my phone up to record," I tell her.

"We'll figure something out." She opens the door, letting me pass through. "What are you going to do about Friday? He won't be happy if I stay in the classroom. I can see him being a jerk and kicking me out."

I shrug as I wrap my coat around me. "I don't know what I'm going to do, but he threatened me in there. He said not to think about missing Friday's lesson, which is what I was thinking about."

"I think we should tell someone. I don't have a good feeling about this."

"I don't either, but we still need proof."

"I know," she says, sighing. "What are we going to do?"

"Are you okay with waiting outside the classroom for me? If he notices, I can say you're my ride home. If that's okay with you."

"Of course, I will. I'm not going to leave you alone with that tosser."

"Emma, wait up." I turn around at the sound of the same voice that got me in trouble. I can't help but narrow my eyes at him when he stops in front of us, pushing his hood off, looking sheepish. "I'm sorry about that back there. He can be a hard-arse. I didn't mean to get you into trouble."

"It's fine," I tell him shortly, still annoyed.

He gives me what I suppose he thinks is a sexy grin, but instead, it makes him look like a serial killer.

"So, I was wondering if you wanted to grab a drink before class on Friday, maybe get something to eat?"

I gape at him. I'm not sure whether I'm more surprised he had the nerve to ask me out after getting me into trouble, or the fact he's asking me out at all. I'd feel flattered, but I'm too pissed at him.

"She won't be going anywhere with you," Banner says, stepping up behind me. I relax against him, my lips tugging into a smile when he wraps his arms around my waist protectively.

"Sorry, mate, didn't know she had a boyfriend."

I don't even know his name, yet he acts like he should know everything about me. I want to scoff, but I keep quiet, not wanting the two to get into a fight.

"Now you do. Run along," Banner orders, his tone hard—scary.

He runs off like someone lit his arse on fire. I turn to Banner, grinning. "Thank you for rescuing me. How did you know I was going to turn him down?"

He grins back, looking too sexy—it should be a sin. "I didn't. I just didn't want someone trying to steal my future wife."

I giggle, rolling my eyes at him. "Stop being silly. Either way, I'm grateful."

"Well, if this isn't awkward…" Becky says. I realise then that Banner and I are standing close to each other—intimately close—both lost in our little bubble. She shuffles on her feet, looking anywhere but at us.

I laugh as Banner chuckles. "Come on, you pair. I'll give you a lift home, Becky. With a killer on the loose, you shouldn't be out alone."

"Are you sure you can prise yourself away from Emma long enough to get in your car?"

He winks at her before sighing dramatically. "It will be tough, Becky—real tough. But the quicker we drop you off, the quicker we're alone," he tells her.

I flush at his suggestive comment but find myself not wanting to correct him—to let her think we're together. She hasn't asked me outright, so I'm not lying.

"You, dawg. Just try to keep your eyes on the road," Becky warns him. "I promised my mum I wouldn't die before I was thirty."

"Thirty? But it's okay after?" Banner asks, giving her a dry look. I have to admit, Becky is a little much, but it's why I like her. You can never predict what she's going to say next.

"She'll probably be gone before then," she states bluntly, before giving him a dry look. "So, you gonna be okay?"

"Always. Precious cargo and all that."

She looks at me, her eyebrows raised. "Is he always so charming?"

I giggle, nodding. "Yep."

"Great!" she mutters, zipping her coat up.

Banner wraps his arm around me, pulling me close. We're nearing his car when I feel someone watching me once again. Discretely, so I don't alert Banner and make him worry, I look around the car park. There's a few people around, one getting into a taxi and another into a car waiting to pick them up, but I don't feel like it was one of them watching me. I scan the area, concerned Darren is out there, probably hoping I'd be alone.

I get frustrated when I don't see anything.

"You gonna get in?"

I jump, glancing away from the dark to Banner's concerned face. "Yeah."

He doesn't need to know I keep feeling like someone is watching me, or that my teacher is making me uncomfortable. He'd want to protect me and probably end up doing something stupid.

And if there is anyone *I* want to protect in my life, it's him. I won't let him risk his degree over me.

Chapter 15

I ignore Banner's questioning stare as I walk around my bed and to my desk to pack my bag. I've been cranky the whole day, fearing and stressing about tonight's class.

Last night we went to bed early. Banner fell asleep next to me within minutes, but after tossing and turning for four hours, I gave up and headed to the living room to finish the novel I've been working on. It gave me the escape I needed, and I managed to fall asleep for a few hours before I woke up to Mark leaving for work.

"Are you okay?"

With my hands on my hips, I spin around to face him. "I said I'm fine. I wish you'd stop asking," I snap, instantly feeling bad. "I'm sorry. I'm tired. I couldn't sleep last night."

His gaze softens. "I know. I heard you leave the room last night."

"Why didn't you say anything?"

"I came to keep you company, but I saw you engrossed in your laptop."

I feel worse hearing that. I've been a bitch to him all day, moody and snappy. "I'm sorry."

"Is there something going on? Is Darren worrying you? If you want, I can talk to him again, tell him to leave you alone."

I walk over to him, crouching down and placing my hands on his thighs. I hate the sad expression on his face. "I'm fine. This isn't about Darren. I'm sorry for being a bitch to you. I'll tell you what's bothering me later. Right now, I just need to find my book before I'm late."

I close my eyes when he runs a finger down my cheek. "I don't care about you snapping at me; I'm a big boy. I'm worried about you. You've not been acting like yourself for a few days." He glances away before staring deeply into my eyes. "Is it because I told that lad you were taken?"

I suck in my bottom lip. I hate lying to him. But I can't let him think it was because of the lad from class. "Banner, I don't even know his name. There is no way I would go out with him. Plus, you said we were getting married," I tease, before being serious. "I promise, after you pick me up, we can come back here, and I will tell you everything."

He cups my cheek, a smile tugging at his lips. "You're the only one I'd marry," he teases—well, I think he is anyway. "And I can wait. Just don't shut me out again."

Breathlessly, I answer. "I won't—I promise."

His eyes darken at the sound of my husky voice, and he leans forward. "You ready?" Levi asks, barging in.

When I would have fallen on my arse, Banner catches my arms, helping me to my feet. I blush, stepping away as I grab my bag.

"Yeah, I'm ready," I tell Levi, before facing Banner. His face is a hard mask, glaring at Levi, but when he sees me, his expressions softens, and he smiles. "I'll see you later?"

"Yep. I'll wait outside, ready for when you finish."

When I step out of the room, my stomach sinks, dread filling me. I glance over my shoulder, torn, something inside of me screaming at me to stay. I ignore it, shaking away the shiver running down my spine, and head out the door, not looking back again.

∼

If I thought life was going to give me a break, I was dead wrong. I prayed Mr. Flint wouldn't be here all day, but my prayers went unanswered when I found him leaning on his desk, looking at me smugly when I walked through the door.

He's passed me a few times during class, brushing his fingers along the back of my neck. I clutched the phone in my hand, wanting to call Banner to come get me. The only thing stopping me is wanting Mr. Flint fired. After Wednesday, I don't think Becky and I are the only girls he's harassed.

We still have ten minutes before class is due to finish. When Mr. Flint walks down the aisle towards the front of the class, the hairs on the back of my neck stand on end. He clears his throat to get everyone's attention, and I jump a little in my seat, feeling on edge when his gaze meets mine.

"Since you've accomplished a lot tonight, I'll let you guys go home early. If anyone has any questions, feel free to email me. You can leave," he says, dismissing the class.

Thinking that means I'm off the hook, I grab my bag, sticking my phone in my pocket. I'm walking behind the others when Mr. Flint steps in front of me, blocking my path and giving me a smug smile. I look over his shoulder, seeing Becky looking worriedly at me just outside the door.

He turns to see who I'm staring at, his eyes narrowing into slits, and I use the opportunity to press record on my phone. He walks over to the door, placing one hand on it. "Goodbye, Becky," he says calmly, shutting it in her face.

I watch her face pale through the tiny window in the door, feeling panic rise in my throat when she moves away. I pray she doesn't go far, a sliver of fear worming its way through my veins when he turns to glare at me, his expression making me take a step back.

"Were you thinking of leaving?"

A flash of yellow passes the window, and I instantly relax. I straighten my spine defiantly as I answer him. "I thought I could go, since you were letting the class leave early."

"You thought wrong," he bites out, stepping closer. "When I tell you to be somewhere, you be there."

Who the hell does he think he is?

"Step away," I warn him, holding my hand up, surprised it's not shaking—like I am inside.

He smirks eerily. "Do I make you nervous, Emma?"

I flinch when he reaches out, swirling a lock of my hair around his finger. "You're a very beautiful girl... until you open that mouth of yours." He drops my hair, his eyes raking up and down my body. I cringe, looking away.

"Did you want to go over my coursework or can I go?" I ask, not comfortable with our plan anymore. It doesn't feel safe, especially when I don't see Becky near the door.

"I had something different in mind. I've seen you watching me," he says softly.

"I'm going. And for the record, I wasn't watching you for the reasons you're thinking. I like to keep an eye on the predator in the room."

He laughs in my face. I step around him, heading for the door, but his grip on my arm stops me. I wince when his fingers dig in, and I know they're going to leave a bruise.

"Don't touch me," I snap shakily, shoving his hand off my arm.

He grins, a look of pure joy passing over his face as his hand goes to my throat. He doesn't squeeze, just pushes me back until I'm forced up against the wall next to the door. My eyes widen as I begin to shake, closing them when memories of Darren come rising to the surface.

Not now.

Please, God, not now.

The visions are gone when I open my eyes, breathing heavily. I grab his wrist, yanking it down. He releases his grip on me, watching me smugly. When I try to move out of his way, he steps with me, his body blocking me. He looks like he's enjoying it, his eyes sparkling.

Just like a hunter after his prey.

"I'm going to have so much fun with you," he whispers breathlessly, stepping closer, practically up against me.

He runs his fingers down my cheek, watching his own movements with rapt fascination.

Once I realise he isn't going to stop, I slap his hand away, my lip trembling. "I said, don't touch me."

He laughs like I just told the funniest joke in the world. He takes a menacing step forward, his expression hardening. My pulse races, but my breath gets trapped in my lungs when he grips my neck in an unyielding grasp. I don't have chance to defend myself. I gasp for breath, my eyes widening when his fingers dig into my throat.

In a blind panic, I lift my hands to his wrist, my fingers digging in as hard as I can manage.

"Little sluts like you thinking they can speak to me that way..." He huffs out a humourless laugh. "When you speak to me, remember who you are talking to. You will respect me." He brings his face closer, his lips nearly brushing mine. I try to look away, but he doesn't let me. "We're going to do something about your teasing. And like a good little girl, you're going to take it."

He loosens his grip, and instead of using it to my advantage and running away, my eyes harden, and I spit in his face.

"Fuck you!" I croak out hoarsely.

"Oh, I will, right after I sort out that dirty mouth of yours."

He brings his hand up, slapping me sharply around the face. I cry out, covering the sting on my cheek, stunned for a moment.

I look into his eyes, seeing a soulless monster staring back at me. I'd never even seen Darren this way—something made from nightmares—and even in them, my brain always woke me up. What I am seeing is what horror movies are made from.

I didn't need to be told twice when my mind screams at me to run. I glance at the door, to the side of me, seeing it so close yet so far away. It's almost touchable. My feet are already moving, heading towards the door as fast as my shaky legs will take me. I don't make it two steps before he's pulling me back by my hair, trapping me against his hard chest.

My heart begins to race so fast I begin to feel the symptoms of a panic attack coming on. I want to be able to close my eyes and wait for someone to save me, but I know it's never going to happen. I'm on my own. Becky was supposed to be outside, but she hasn't come.

She's gone.

Banner will come.

I don't want to deal with what is happening. Not again. I barely survived the first time when Darren attacked me.

A choked cry for help forces itself up my throat, but nothing but a rasp of air escapes. I feel completely paralyzed with fear. I should fight, run away, but the tighter he squeezes me against his chest, the more I feel detached from my own body, utterly terrified that he's going to kill me.

"Where are you going, Emma? I'm not finished. You tease me every week for two hours. Now you're going to learn a lesson, but not before you satisfy me. If you please me, I might go easy with your punishment," he growls, his breath on my ear as he pins my arms to my chest. I struggle harder, a tear falling down my cheek when he licks my earlobe.

"Get off me," I cry out, my eyes on the door, pleading for Becky to walk in and save me.

His one hand grips my wrists to my chest, while the other slides down my chest to my stomach. Bile rises in my throat, but I swallow it back down, kicking him in the shin as he reaches the band of my jeans, his fingers teasing the waistband. He steps back with a hiss before he grips my hair once more, throwing me backwards. I put my hand out to stop the fall, but I land too hard, and I feel the burning pain in my wrist before crying out in agony.

I look up, blowing the hair out of my face, terrified of what will happen next. He storms over, his hands clenched into fists, and I begin to tremble, clutching my arm to my chest.

He kicks out, and I roll over from the force, grunting in pain, one I know all too well from when Darren broke a couple of ribs. I try to breathe, but the stabbing feeling in my ribs makes it hard.

Another kick to the back has me rolling on my front, coughing so hard I can't scream out from the pain. I feel him bend down next to me, pressing my face into the hard, cold floor before spinning me around to face him and straddling me.

"Bitches like you need to learn the hard way. I'm going to enjoy this," he whispers, his eyes glowing.

I struggle to breathe but manage to get out, "Fuck you."

The punch he lands on the corner of my mouth has me spitting out blood. I feel weak, my vision blurring from the pain in not only my wrist but my ribs. The second punch has me drifting in and out. When I look up, fighting to stay awake, he has his fist raised. I blink when the weight of him on me is gone, finding him no longer above me.

Feeling weak, I let my head flop to the side. I struggle to get up when I see Banner punching Mr. Flint in the face—repeatedly.

He's saved me.

"Emma, it's going to be okay. I've called the police. They're going to send an ambulance, too," Becky whispers. I don't look at her, unable to keep my eyes off Banner as he falls back from the punch Mr. Flint managed to get in.

I cry out, feeling a tear fall down my cheek, the sting bringing all the pain back. "Banner," I croak out, feeling weaker by the second.

Distracted by the sound of my voice, Mr. Flint manages to kick Banner in the stomach before getting up and rushing out of the room.

From the look on Banner's face, I can tell he's ready to go after him. "Banner."

He drags his attention from the door Mr. Flint just escaped through and looks at me. His hair is a mess, and his T-shirt is torn and pulled, hanging off his shoulder.

He crawls over to me, his expression filled with anguish and pain. "Emma, what did he do to you?" His hand shakily hovers over my head, his eyes watering. "Where does it hurt?"

"I—" I lick my dry lips, tasting the coppery tang of blood, trying to grasp the words I want to say, but my tongue feels heavy and my vision begins to blur.

"Stay awake, Emma," he warns. "You need to stay awake."

"It—it hurts," I croak out, before coughing, choking on the blood that fills my mouth from the gash on my lip.

"I know, baby, but you need to stay awake. Do it for me, please."

I'd do anything for him.

I love him.

And despite the pain, despite the roaring in my ears as I battle to stay awake, my heart soars as I swear I hear him say, "I love you too."

I want to hold him, needing to know he's ok and yearning to feel him against me. I raise my arms to do just that, when blinding pain lashes through my side, and I pass out.

Chapter 16

Some of the shock from tonight has worn off. My mind, deep down, understands I was attacked, that I'm hurt, whilst a part of me still can't believe it happened. It doesn't feel real, or that it happened only hours ago.

Slowly, I try to sit up, but quickly realise how futile it is when a sharp pain shoots through my ribs. Spots flash behind my eyes and I bite my lip to keep from crying out and showing Banner and Mark how much pain I'm really in. If they make me stay a second longer in this hospital, they're going to need to sedate me. I just want to go home and curl up in bed.

"Here, let me," Banner says softly, helping me up. I swing my legs over the bed, before stopping to catch my breath.

"Thank you."

"I don't think this is a good idea," Mark tells us from where he's pacing.

I look over at him, trying not to cry at his appearance. He looks like he's aged ten years, and he can barely look at me. I don't blame him, either. I caught sight of myself in the mirror, and it's not pretty.

"Mark, I just want to go home."

"You're in pain. You need to be here where they can help you."

"There isn't anything they can do that you can't. Please, just get me out of here. I hate hospitals."

He nods but still doesn't seem convinced. He glances at Banner, his jaw tight. "I'm going to go see what's taking Levi so long. He said he'd call when he's outside."

Banner nods and moves to kneel in front of me, sliding my shoes on my feet. Finally alone, I place my hand on his shoulder, getting his attention. The torment in his eyes has me closing mine briefly. "Are you okay?"

"Yeah. I will be. I'm just pissed right now, Emma. Why didn't you come to me?"

I blink back tears, not needing to hear how stupid and naive I was in thinking I could deal with this on my own.

"Honestly?"

"It's all I ever want from you."

I wince, even though I know he didn't say that to be mean. "I didn't want you to get into a fight. At first, I thought I was just being jumpy because of my past, but then he got in my personal space again. I didn't want to be the reason a man got fired from his job because of my paranoia. I wouldn't be able to live with myself."

"What happened after?"

I look at him straight on. "I was a fool. When I found out he was the same with Becky, we decided to get proof. She already said uni wouldn't believe me; his parents gave too much money to the school. We had a plan to record what he was saying to us, so they'd have no choice but to fire him."

His jaw hardens. "I know. I gave the police your phone." He runs a frustrated hand through his hair. "But you still should have come to me, Emma. Do you know how hard it was not to kill him when I walked into that room? I never want to see that ever again."

A sob bubbles up my throat. "I'm sorry. I'm so fucking sorry. I didn't think it would get this far. I thought I'd record his suggestive remarks and be done with it. I'm sorry."

"Hey, please don't cry," he says, moving my head to lie on his shoulder. "Next time just let me protect you."

"I will. I don't think I can go through something like this again. I wouldn't survive," I admit. "Have they arrested him?"

He pulls back, standing up. "No. They can't find him."

Shaking, I look away, not wanting to register his words and what they mean. "Where's Becky gone?"

"She got picked up by her dad an hour ago. She felt bad about leaving you."

My eyes flash. "She left me?"

He steps closer, helping me to my feet. "When she heard you beg him not to touch you, she looked through the window of the door and saw his hand on your throat. She came running out to the carpark to find me." He pauses, rubbing the back of his neck and inhaling. "I heard a fucking noise and went to investigate it."

"What?" I ask.

He stares down at me, his eyes filled with pain. "I heard a noise in the bushes and went to see what it was. I kept thinking Darren was there. I didn't see Becky until she started heading back inside. I heard her crying and knew something was wrong. When she explained what was happening and that she was on the phone to the police, I ran in to help you."

"You saved me," I tell him, feeling breathless. "Again."

He grins, but I can tell it's forced by the tight lines across his forehead. "We really should get me my own cape."

I giggle, then wince from the pain in my ribs. He didn't break them, but they are badly bruised and will take a few weeks to mend. My wrist, on the other hand, is definitely broken, and I'll have to keep the cast on for six weeks.

"You would look good in tights."

"I'd look good in anything."

I blush, because he would. Even with a busted lip and torn clothes, he looks good. I look at him intently, taking his hand with my good one, and lick my lips. "Thank you for tonight. Thank you for always been there and protecting me."

His expression softens. "I didn't really do a good job."

I shake my head at his words. "I knew you'd come. I knew it. And you did. So, get used to the fact that you're my hero."

A cloud of lust flashes through his eyes. "I'll always be there for you. Always."

He steps closer, bending down until we're eye level. The tension between us is crippling. I want to pull him closer and devour him, but I also want him to be the first to make a move. I'm just going to follow his lead.

"He's ready," Mark interrupts, stepping into the room, causing both Banner and I to groan.

"Okay," I croak out, letting Banner lead me to the wheelchair.

I lean on Banner with a heavy sigh as he helps me up the flight of stairs. With each step, black dots dance in my vision from the pressure that shoots through my bruised ribs. By the time we reach the top, I'm sweating, in excruciating pain, and just want to go to bed.

"Put her on the sofa," Mark fusses, heading for the kitchen.

"I just want to go to bed," I complain.

He pauses before the kitchen, turning to glare at me. "You'll do as your told. The doctor said you need to eat with your medication, and unless you want to wait until morning to take some more pain meds, you'll eat something."

Mutely, I nod, letting Banner steer me over to the sofa. Levi quickly places some pillows behind me to prop me up.

"Do you need anything else?"

"I think Mark has it covered," I whisper, glancing towards the kitchen. He's been distant, barely even looking at me. "He's so mad at me."

Gently, Levi takes one of my hands. "He's mad at himself, Em. Not you."

"Huh?"

He forces a small smile. "He's mad he couldn't protect you," he says, before briefly looking towards the kitchen, where Mark is banging around. "He spent years not being able to protect you. He not only hates his parents, but yours too. When we first got together he would tell me about them, about how he wanted you to live with him. But you were finishing school, and then everything happened. He would spend hours on the phone to your grandparents, trying to get them to talk you into moving here."

I wipe a lone tear. "They did. They gave me the option of either moving in with them, or here, with Mark." I give a sad smile, remembering that low time in my life. "I chose Mark. He was always there for me as a kid. We were both the black sheep of the family."

"It was hard for him. He was kicked out, not forced to stay—like you. He hasn't said anything, but he feels guilty about tonight. He was hoping with you here to watch over, he would be able to prevent anything bad from happening to you."

"That's stupid. He couldn't have known what was going to happen any more than I could have. He shouldn't feel responsible for me."

"He loves you," he tells me softly, something I already know.

"I love him too. I feel terrible for putting you all through this."

"Don't," Mark croaks from the doorway, holding a bowl with steam coming from it. "I should have been there for you."

I don't take my eyes off him as he walks into the room, dropping the bowl on the table before leaning down next to Levi, placing his hand over my cast.

"I'm sorry."

I don't know what else to say. I feel awful for what they are all feeling. If I had been honest from the start, maybe we could have prevented this from happening, made a different plan to get the proof we needed to report Mr. Flint.

"Don't be. I'm the one who's sorry. I've been a wanker all night." Tears gather in his eyes. "Just let me look after you. I don't want to hear any moaning, either."

I strain out a chuckle, glad the tension has eased some. "I won't; I promise."

"Good. I'm going to get you some clean clothes to put on."

My eyes widen in horror. "Um, I can do that," I tell him, not wanting my cousin going through my drawers.

Levi stands, chuckling. "I'll go do it. When you're up tomorrow, I'll help you shower."

"No, you won't," Banner blurts out.

Levi raises his eyebrow. "I'm gay."

"I don't fucking care. I'll help her," Banner tells him.

"Banner, it's fine," I tell him, blushing. There is no way I'm letting Banner wash me.

He doesn't look happy, but he nods. "Okay. But wear a bikini."

I try to force myself not to smile, but it's useless. I end up beaming, wincing when my cut lip cracks.

"Eat your soup and I'll be back," Levi says, smirking at Banner.

Mark hands me the bowl, and although I'm not hungry, I know I won't be able to handle being sick if I take the tablets on an empty stomach.

"I'm gonna go ring the police station to see if they have any updates. I don't trust the fuckers to call back. They've got a shit ton of stuff going on with the murders. I want to make sure they're doing their job," Banner says grimly.

"I'm sure they are," I assure him.

"We'll see," he says absently. "I'm also going to let the lads know I won't be coming in this week, and I'll tell my teachers too."

I tense. "Banner, you can't miss classes because of me."

He gives me a dry look. "Don't argue, otherwise I'll take two weeks off."

I pout, scooping soup onto my spoon. "Whatever." He gets up to leave, when I remember something. "Do they know when I can get my belongings back? I want to check on Becky."

"I'm not sure. I'll ask when I speak to them. And I've got Becky's number. You can text her after you've taken your tablets."

I nod my agreement before going back to my soup, listening to Mark move towards the kitchen before coming back with my prescription bag.

"It says to take one at night on this one, and one three times daily on this one. Once you've finished, take them both and then I'll leave them on the kitchen side for you."

"Thank you, Mark—for everything."

"I'll do anything for you, Emma."

"I see that."

"Good," he tells me softly, running his hand down my hair.

Tonight, I got lucky. My attack could have been worse, much worse, and I shudder to think how far Mr. Flint planned to go.

When Darren said in court he wasn't going to rape me, I didn't know what to believe. But after tonight, seeing the look in Mr. Flint's eyes, I'm a hundred percent positive that he wasn't. The two were completely different. Darren attacked me out of anger and because his mind was clouded from drugs. Mr. Flint, however, attacked me out of some warped need for power. He wanted me to feel weak and vulnerable, and he preyed on it.

I'm glad to be at home, safe and surrounded by those I love. It's a reminder to me that I'm not alone. That, together, they will help me through this, so I don't go back to that dark, lonely place.

This is what love is.

What family is.

And I'm not going to let someone take that away from me. Not now, not ever.

Chapter 17

The past few days have been a blur. With the painkillers in my system, I've mostly slept. Today is the first day I've not taken one, hating the effects they have on me.

"I'll only be gone an hour. Are you sure there isn't anything you want me to get you?"

I narrow my eyes at my cousin. His heart is in the right place, and I love him for everything he's done, but I'm mad at him for telling my grandparents what happened to me. Now he's worried them for nothing.

They are coming down today for a visit and to check on me. I'm also annoyed at all the fussing. I can't even take a piss without one of them standing guard. No joke. Levi either takes me or Banner does, thinking I'm incapable. It's got to the point that I'm ready to kill one of them.

"Mark, I'm fine. Nan and Granddad should be here soon, so you'd better get going if you want to be back for them in time."

"I just don't want to leave you. I can get someone to cover my shift."

I roll my eyes. "Just go. Both Banner and Levi are here, and they aren't going anywhere."

"I just don't like that he's still out there."

I look down at my lap, fiddling with the spine of the book I'm reading. "I know. I don't like it either."

"Hey, it will be fine—they'll find him," he says softly, coming to sit down next to me on the bed.

When I look up, a frown is marring his forehead, but I say what I do because it's what I'm feeling. "I doubt that. They can't even find the killer who is murdering all those girls. He's probably long gone."

Mark sighs. "For his sake, he'd better be. Because if I don't kill him, Banner and Levi will."

I chuckle, glad the pain in my chest is easing off. "Word."

He rolls his eyes at me before getting up, patting my knee. "I won't be long."

I watch him leave with a tightness in my chest. I've been worried that Mr. Flint will hurt those around me because I went to the police.

One thing is for sure, me and Becky weren't the only girls. Since I reported him, more girls have stepped forward, all claiming the same thing. Thankfully, no one was raped, but a few said it had been close. And from what the police officer was telling us, he always preyed on quiet, shy girls, believing they would keep their mouths closed.

He was right, and he was wrong. It only takes one person to stand up to predators like him and then everyone speaks up.

My bedroom door swings open and I look up from the book to see Banner step inside. "Who was at the door?" I ask, knowing he left to answer it. Levi was in the shower and Mark refused to leave. My stomach sinks when he frowns, looking torn. "Banner?"

He clears his throat, sitting on the edge of the bed next to me. "It was Jordan and two other girls. They heard the rumour about Mr. Flint and came to see you. It's not just your case they are after him for questioning."

"What do you mean?" I ask, feeling sick. I rub across my stomach, wishing the ache would go.

"Jordan said her friend was taken in to hospital the night of your attack. Someone gave her medication that caused her to have a miscarriage."

"What?" I yell, trying to sit up straighter but failing. Banner helps me, fluffing the cushion behind my head.

"She lost the baby."

"Why do they think Mr. Flint is involved?" I already know the answer, but I need to hear it.

"He was doing the same thing to the girl who miscarried. She was a student of his and he made her feel uncomfortable. They heard what happened and wanted to come and see if you were okay."

"Why didn't you let them in?" I'm still shocked at the horrendous acts he's committed.

"Because I didn't want them getting you worked up. As soon as they explained what had happened, I knew it would only upset you. I told them to pop round in a week or so when you're better."

"Banner, you should have let them in. Jordan's been a good friend since I got here."

He looks guilty for a moment, before it's gone. "Sorry. Plus, your grandparents are coming today. Jordan can come over any other time."

I give him a dry look before nodding. "All right, I'll drop it. But a few minutes wouldn't have hurt you."

"I hardly get you to myself as it is. I'm done sharing," he tells me, causing me to giggle.

Thinking of Jordan reminds me of Becky. I've not heard from her since the night Mr. Flint attacked me. I miss her and want to know if she's okay.

"Have you spoken to Becky?" I whisper.

His expression saddens. "No, but I did speak to her dad. He said she hasn't been doing so good. She feels responsible for your attack. She keeps telling them she should have gone in to help you instead of running outside."

I scrunch my face up. "If she hadn't, he could have hurt her, and neither of us would have gotten help. She did the right thing."

"I told her dad that, too. It still turns my stomach to think what could have happened. If she hadn't of got me…"

I place my hand over his. "Hey, it's okay. What's done is done. There is no going back."

"Yeah," he chokes out hoarsely.

"I've texted her a few times but she's not replying. Once some of this has blown over, we'll see if her dad will let us visit. That okay?"

"I think that's a great idea. If she's thinking the way she is, she probably feels too ashamed to face you."

"You're probably right."

A tap on the door interrupts us, and Levi pokes his head inside. "Your nan and granddad are here."

I groan, falling back against my pillows. "I'll be out in a minute."

"I got the loveseat ready for you," Levi tells me, before addressing

Banner. "Just bring her blanket out. It's cold as shit today and I don't want her catching a chill."

When he leaves, Banner helps me up from the bed. I'm still stiff from the bruises and aches in my back and chest but moving around is easier than it was before.

"I swear, I have two dads in this house," I mutter under my breath.

"I hope I'm not included in that," Banner says, his voice high-pitched.

I glance over at him as I slide my feet into my slippers, winking at him. "Oh, the last thing I want to call you is daddy."

His eyes widen at my flirting before a smirk crosses his lips. "Well, in the bedroom you can call me whatever you want."

I laugh, clutching myside when it hurts a little. "Thanks —I think."

"Pleasure," he says, chuckling. He holds his arm up and I tuck mine around it, letting him lead me out into the living area.

Gasps echo around the room as soon as I enter. I look up, finding my nan with tears in her eyes, her hand over mouth, watching me. She looks devastated, broken.

"Nan, I'm fine. I swear," I tell her, glancing to my granddad for help. He looks furious, his hands clenched tightly and his jaw solid. His gaze turns hard as he turns to Levi. "Are you sure you don't know where he is? I have a right mind to get my hunting rifle and shoot the fucker."

I gasp at my granddad's words. "Granddad!" He's never violent. Ever. Seeing this side of him is shocking. Banner chuckles at him, and when my granddad narrows his eyes at him, he shuts up, standing straighter.

"And you, boy. You'd better take care of my girl, otherwise I'll shoot *you*."

God, someone shoot *me*.

"Granddad, stop it."

"Oh my, Emma. Look what he did to you," my nan cries, stepping forward to hug me. She barely touches me, probably too afraid of my injuries. When she pulls back, a few tears slip free. "Maybe you should come stay with us on the farm. You grandfather is right. He has a rifle he can protect you with."

I roll my eyes. "That thing hasn't been used for a long time, ever since they banned fox hunting fourteen years ago. He's more likely to shoot himself."

"I'll have you know I still take it out every now and again. We have a few pheasants on our land that need a little warning."

I'd laugh at his expression, but I don't want to hurt his feelings. "All right, all right. But I'm not coming to stay with you. I really like it here."

My nan takes me in, a small smile spreading on her wrinkled face. "You do look different. You're glowing again."

"You'd better not be pregnant," my granddad booms, staring daggers at Banner.

Banner, ever the soldier, just shakes his head, looking bored. Levi, on the other hand, drops the cup of tea in his hand.

"You're pregnant?"

Banner chuckles. "No, she's not. Chill."

"Oh," Levi says, looking gutted before heading back into the kitchen.

"Good. I want my grandchild married first, just like we were."

Banner nods, not saying anything. Me? I want to die of embarrassment. I glance at my nan, pleading with her to change the subject.

She doesn't.

"He's right. And you'd make such a beautiful bride."

"Me and Banner aren't together," I squeak out.

"Yet," Banner mutters, looking away when I glance at him.

"Let's sit down. You can tell us everything that happened," Nan says, walking me over to the loveseat.

Levi comes back with two more cups of coffee and a roll of kitchen paper under his arm. "Would you like one?" he asks me.

"Please."

He looks at Banner, who nods. "Coffee. Easy on the coffee this time. I couldn't sleep for a week after the last one you made."

Levi chuckles. "I didn't make it. Mark did."

We all wince, and noticing our expressions, Banner looks at us warily. "What?"

"Never let Mark make you coffee," I tell him.

"I couldn't sleep for a month straight after he made me one once," Granddad chimes in.

"Mine was so thick I couldn't swallow it," Nan adds.

"Doesn't have trouble with other things," Granddad mutters, looking away when she slaps his chest.

"Oh, you."

I'm going to be sick.

"Why didn't either of you say anything?" Banner asks, looking slightly annoyed.

"I didn't know he made you one," I tell him, although I might not have warned him if I had. It's funny to see how people will react. Lake was so hyper one time, it took medication to calm her down.

"I thought you knew." Levi shrugs, but I can see he's lying.

"Fucker," Banner mutters when Levi leaves for the kitchen.

"Right, tell us what happened and what the police are doing to catch this son of a bitch," my granddad orders, before looking at Banner with a questioning gaze. "Then after, you can tell me what your intentions are with my grandchild."

"Only good—"

Granddad holds his hand up, stopping Banner before he can finish. "After."

When he looks at me, I shrink back into my cushions, smiling my thanks when Banner tucks the blanket over me.

I explain everything that happened leading up to the attack, and my plan. I don't go much into the attack, already telling the police what happened enough times already. Instead, I tell them of my injuries, and some of the things he said to me when he had me.

"Have the police got no leads?" Granddad asks, looking worried.

Banner is the one to answer. "They are looking into it, but so far, they can't find him. They've got ads on Facebook, the papers and everything, since he has ties to Wales and Scotland. They want to make sure it's spread over that area in case he decides to escape there. Hopefully, if anyone recognises him, they'll call the helpline."

"And he's done this to other girls?" Nan asks, her shaking hand above her heart.

I nod sadly. "Yeah. Once it got out about me, more students, present and past, stepped forward, telling the police their stories. Most of the girls either left or dropped his class before it got as far as it did. So far, no one has come forward that he sexually assaulted them."

"What on earth were the university thinking? Surely one of those girls reported him."

I can hear Banner's teeth grind together. "Two girls did, but because of the funding his family donated to the university, they swept it under the rug, saying there wasn't enough evidence and it was their word against his."

"He needs to be shot," Granddad growls.

I'm still getting used to this side of him. He's usually really laid back.

"I've written a letter to the university board panel, wanting answers myself. I've also told them I want your tuition money refunded, that you weren't paying to be assaulted or sexually harassed."

"Nan," I whine.

"I don't want to hear it. They seemed more than happy to refund you. And when you're ready to go back, you are welcome. If they say anything different, you come to me."

I relax, knowing I won't have to give up my course, but feel sad because I know there is no way I'll be able to go back to doing night courses.

"I might start doing part-time classes in the day. I don't think I could go back there at night."

Her expression softens. "That's understandable, darling. Whenever you are ready to decide, I will help you sort it out."

"Thank you. I might wait until September and enrol then. I want to get used to being around a lot of people."

"If anyone can do it, you can," she tells me, her eyes shining.

"Thank you."

"And we have that camping trip in a few weeks. You can get used to a small group first and work your way up."

I smile at Banner. "That sounds like a great idea."

"I'm full of them," he tells me, winking.

"You're full of something," Granddad mutters.

"Granddad," I moan, rolling my eyes at him.

"Sorry." He doesn't look sorry. "Where's Mark?"

"He just had to—" The key entering the lock has me pausing, glancing at the door. "Here he is."

As soon as he walks in, they engulf him in hugs and kisses. My grandparents were the only people in our family who didn't care that he was gay. They loved him no matter what, just like family are meant to.

"Does your granddad really have a gun?" Banner whispers in my ear.

I shiver, facing him. "He has three, but the other two are more for show."

His face turns a deathly pale colour. "Fuck!"

"Right then, boy," Granddad booms, coming to sit back down. "Now you can tell me what your intentions are with my girl."

I bite back a smile when Banner whimpers, trying to appear as small as possible. I simply shrug, giving him a 'go on' look and try so hard to not give in when he gives me those puppy dog eyes.

I glance around the room at my family, feeling so much love. It feels good having us all together.

And I hope we have more times like this together in the future.

Because right here, right now, this is my family, my everything. And I don't want to lose that.

Chapter 18

Two weeks have flown by with no word from Mr. Flint. The police are no closer to finding him, but they did manage to catch the killer murdering those poor innocent girls. It's been all over the news, every station covering the story.

Two people were held against their will before they had no choice but to kill the lad. It terrifies me to know he went to the same university as me. He even worked at the library. The times I visited the library I never saw another male working there, and I'm kind of glad. I have enough going in my life right now to feel freaked out over being in the presence of a real-life murderer.

I inhale, running my sweaty palms down my coat. Banner is going to be here any second with his friends. The only reason I'm not backing out of going is because I don't want to let him down. In the time I've been here, he's been nothing but be good to me. Instead of going out partying like lads his age do, he's stayed in with me and kept me company. He's taken me to his favourite places, taken me to watch movies. He's been content for it to be just us. Backing out of this weekend would disappoint him, even though he wouldn't say anything. It's just who he is.

"He's here," Mark tells me when Banner's car pulls down our road.

My knees begin to shake when he pulls up to the curb and jumps out. His friend, who's sitting in the passenger seat, gets out too.

I look between them, feeling jittery. I rub my arms, waiting for Banner to reach me before speaking.

I also can't help but admire him. He looks hot today, wearing his faded jeans, white crisp T-shirt and grey zip-up hoody with a leather jacket over the top.

Holy crap, he looks fine today.

"Hey," I greet breathlessly.

He winks, taking my bag from the floor. "Is this everything?"

I nod. "Yeah."

"Mate, I can see why you've been hiding her from us. She's hot as fuck." I glance at his friend who had spoken, heating rising up my neck and cheeks.

"Tom?" Banner says, exasperated. "Shut the fuck up."

I giggle, glancing away when Banner gives me a look.

"I bet he didn't want us to meet 'cause he knew you'd run away with me," Tom says, ignoring the glare Banner sends him. "I'm Tom, by the way. The good-looking and clever one."

"Emma," I tell him, waving.

He grins. "Cute."

"All right, let's get this show on the road. We've still got to pick up Connor and the girls."

"Girls?" I ask, first I'm hearing of this.

"Yeah, they found a couple of girls to come so they wouldn't be alone with only each other's company," Banner explains.

"Okay." I just hope they're nice. One thing I've learnt is that girls can be mean when it comes to lads. Lake and I learnt the hard way at school. If a lad showed interest in either of us, they'd attack us like vultures. They were relentless, not giving up until the lad moved on.

"Come on, you can sit in the front. Those fuckers can sit in the back."

"Wait, there won't be room if you pick up the girls and Connor," I tell him.

"John is picking up one of the girls for us. We're gonna meet them there," he assures me.

"That's good, then. I wouldn't want you to get pulled over."

"Keep an eye on her," Mark warns Banner. He holds the door for me, but I stop before getting in. "And be careful. If you want to come home, call me. Okay?"

"I will; I promise," I tell him, bending down to get in. I'm stopped mid-way when Levi calls out to me.

"Wait, you forgot your pillow."

I blush when Tom starts laughing behind me from the backseat. "Thanks, Levi." I grab the pillow, clutching it to my chest.

"Did you tell her to call us if she wants to come home?" Levi asks Mark quietly, making me smile.

"Yeah."

"Did you charge your phone?" Levi then asks me.

I roll my eyes, my lips twitching with amusement. "I did. Now go, it's cold out here."

They both look reluctant to let me go, Mark looking seconds away from carrying me over his shoulder back into the flat.

"Okay, we'll see you when you get back," Levi tells me, stepping close Mark and wrapping his arm around him.

"Take care of her," Mark warns over the hood of the car.

"I will," Banner replies.

Mark shuts my door after I get in. I wave goodbye to them, chuckling quietly at their sad, pouty faces.

"Brothers?" Tom asks, leaning forward in his chair.

Blindly, Banner slaps him back, looking in the rear-view mirror. "Sit the fuck back and put your belt on."

"Yes, Dad."

Smiling at his teasing, I answer him. "No. Mark's my cousin and Levi's his boyfriend."

Tom starts choking. "They're gay?"

I narrow my eyes, pissed. He doesn't sound judgemental, but you can never know. When I look at Banner, he doesn't even blink, not seeming fazed.

"Yes. Why?"

"It's a shame they aren't single. My brother needs to get laid. He has shit taste when it comes to men."

I relax when it's clear he doesn't have a problem with them being a couple. Well, not for the reasons I presumed.

"Sorry. I could ask them if they have any gay friends who are single, if you want."

"Yeah. They can't be arseholes though. Nathan let his last boyfriend walk all over him. Pissed me off."

"I bet," I tell him quietly, feeling the tension ease from my body.

"So, mate, what are we going to tell Coach when the organisers tell them we brought girls with us?" Tom asks.

"You didn't tell me there would people working there."

Banner looks at me from the corner of his eye. "Yeah. They keep the place clean and shit. There's showers, toilets, a mini café that closes around eleven, and a store that sells essentials for those who forget stuff."

"Don't need the café, though. I brought some steaks. Throw them on the barbie and we're good to go."

"Sounds yummy," I murmur, hoping one of them know how to cook.

We pull up outside another house and Banner blares his horn. I wince, wishing he could have warned me so I could cover my ears.

A guy, who I presume is Connor, walks out with a girl in tow, his expression miserable. He gets in the car, sliding over to the middle to give room to the girl he's with.

"Hey, guys," he says, sounding as miserable as he looks.

"Do you guys know if there will be bugs? Or if they have some hand sanitizer? I've only got a small bottle and Connor said they'll be a shop there."

I watch Banner open his mouth to answer, but the girl continues without taking a breath. "And I won't have to go on long walks or anything, right? I don't want my feet to dry up or crack. With the cold, it's been hard to keep them soft. Oh, and I can't drink anything but bottled water, so I hope they don't pour it from the tap."

"Kelsea, seriously, just stop talking for five minutes," Connor moans.

My eyes widen at his bluntness, but Kelsea doesn't seem affected. "I need to work my vocal cords. My singing instructor said I should concentrate on talking instead of singing for a bit."

"Probably wanted to stop you singing," I hear muttered.

"What?"

"Probably couldn't believe his ears," Connor says loudly.

Her giggle has me resting the pillow against the window and covering both of my ears for a second. God, it's screechy. And loud.

"He told me I had a sinful voice," she tells him sweetly.

Banner struggles to concentrate on the road when he bursts out laughing. I flick his thigh, shushing him quietly.

"I just bet he did," Connor mutters. "Hey, you're the chick who stole Banner. How you doing?"

Not wanting to be rude, I turn in my seat and smile. "Hi, I'm Emma."

His eyes widen, going from me to Banner. "Bro, I can see why the fuck you've been hiding her. Were you that scared I'd steal her from you? She's fucking hot."

Blushing, I turn around in my seat, watching the cars pass us by.

"Shut up, Connor. And you can't steal what belongs to me."

Warmth fills my chest at his words, feeling love seep through me. He takes my good hand in his, resting it on his thigh as he drives.

"It's probably all of the layers she's wearing," Kelsea pipes in.

"What?" Connor asks, sounding puzzled.

"You said she was hot. I just meant if she took a few layers off, she wouldn't be."

Connor laughs, sounding genuine and relaxed. "She can take as many layers as she wants off," he says suggestively, making me blush.

Banner's hand squeezes mine for a second before releasing it. "Bro, unless you want me to pull over and lay you out in front of your girl, I suggest you shut up."

"She's not my girl," he blurts out, causing Banner and Tom to start laughing.

"I'm his *woman*. Girl makes me sound five. And how cool is this trip! I wasn't sure about going camping; I've never been. But Connor explained it's luxury at its finest and I couldn't resist. While you guys do guy stuff, I'm gonna go get a wax, maybe a pedi and massage done at the spa."

"Um, it's not that kind of—"

"Bro, I wouldn't bother unless you want to drive back," Connor interrupts Tom.

"She's doesn't know it's not—"

Connor coughs, interrupting Banner. "Bro, I said don't."

"I'm so excited. This is going to be the best weekend ever," Kelsea gushes, completely oblivious to what's being said.

I look out the window, away from Banner. It will only take one look for me to burst out laughing. I don't want Kelsea to think I'm laughing at her.

~

We pull into a carpark outside a building, which I think is the reception, a gift shop, a tiny food shop/off-licence, and a café.

Pulling to a stop, we all get out of the car. I stretch my back, groaning at the crack that feels so good after sitting down for so long.

"Um, Connor, where's the spa?"

Connor pops his head out of the boot, grimacing. "I just need to set up a tent. We'll talk later," he tells her.

She pouts, looking around with a puzzled expression. "A real tent?"

"A real tent!" Tom yells, looking ready to strangle her. She did spend the drive yapping everyone's ear off.

"I thought you were joking. I know how much you love to tease me. I can't sleep on the floor. It's not good for my back. I need a real bed."

"Babe, don't worry, I have an air mattress to blow up."

The look she gives him has me stepping back, bumping into Banner. "Sorry," I whisper, unable to look away.

He wraps his arm around my waist, watching along with me. "This should be fun. Three, two, one—"

"I am not sleeping on something so… so… tacky," she screeches, stomping her foot. "Go book us a room at a hotel. Preferably five stars."

"You can sleep on the floor if that's what you want, but I'm sleeping on the air mattress. I paid twenty quid for it. And there aren't any hotels around here, babe. Just chill. You'll love it; you'll see."

"I can't believe this is happening to me. I'll be back in a minute. I need to call my therapist," she tells him, before stomping off.

Tom glares at Connor. "Bro, *I'm* gonna have to book an appointment to see one by the end of this weekend. What were you thinking?"

Connor throws his hands up. "I was thinking she has great tits."

Tom scoffs, disgusted. "And the mouth is worth it?"

"She's not that bad," Connor tells him, but doesn't sound so convinced himself.

Tom glances at us. "I'm sleeping next to you two—far away from those two. And if I disappear, follow me. I'm probably trying to hang myself from a tree."

I place my hand over my mouth to smother the giggle.

"I'll go talk to her," Connor murmurs, his shoulders slumping.

Banner waits for him to leave before laughing. "He's gonna end up ditching her before the weekend is up."

"I'll take that bet, but I'll raise you: he'll drown her before it's up."

"You two are bad," I tell them, giggling.

Banner takes my hand, dragging me towards the boot. "Let's get these tents and go set up. The others are already here."

"Okay."

Chapter 19

When Banner said we would be going camping with his friends, I felt kind of anxious. It's been a long time since I was surrounded by a group of friends, let alone been included with them. I wasn't sure where I would fit in, but in one night, I've come to like every single one of them, even the girls they brought along. Most of the girls already knew each other, but it didn't stop them from including me. One girl—Sammy—has been the only one to give me the cold shoulder, but she hasn't been nasty about it.

I've seen the looks she's sent Banner when she thinks we aren't looking, so I can't blame her for being pissed. It's clear as day that she has a thing for him, even though she came with Ross.

I let the looks go because if roles were reversed, I'd be sending her evil looks too.

Last night was kind of rowdy, but it wasn't as overwhelming as I thought it would be. We had fun and it was nice meeting all of Banner's friends.

Today, they spent the day doing activities, whilst me and Kelsea watched on. Kelsea didn't want to get dirty or break a nail, whereas I watched with envy, cursing my broken arm.

It's getting dark out as Tom starts another fire—or tries to. The timid girl, who is dating Tom, pushes him to the side, lighting it herself.

"How do you do that?" he growls. Bless his heart, he's been trying for at least twenty minutes. The night before it was late before he finally let her have a go, and within minutes, she had one going.

I turn to Ross, who is flipping burgers, annihilating them until they break up. He growls, making me giggle as he throws on some fresh ones.

I snuggle up to Banner on the chair, since some of the lads forgot to bring spares. The only other place is the ground or on a tree trunk that has been cut down. And there is no way I'm freezing my arse off.

I'm already cold enough. Plus, cuddling up to Banner is my favourite thing ever. He's also toasty warm.

"You having fun?" he whispers.

"The best. You have great friends," I tell him, watching as Connor shoves Ross away from the barbeque when he nearly breaks up the last lot of burgers we have.

"They're okay," he chuckles. "Want to go for a walk after we've eaten?"

"Yeah, sounds good," I tell him. "God, it's cold tonight." I rub my gloved hands together.

"It's supposed to warm up in a few weeks. Though I don't see how when it's this cold."

I give him a dry look. "It's England, anything can happen."

He chuckles. "Word!"

"Food's ready," Connor yells to the group.

"I can't eat any more meat. Is there any salad?" Kelsea whines from the chair she's sitting in, a blanket covering her legs.

"No!" everyone but me and Banner shout. The argument last night was over the burgers being cheap ones. She whined for a whole hour, refusing to eat them. Once it was clear Connor wasn't going to go find her something else to eat, she made him light up another bag of coal.

She shrinks into her chair. "All right."

Banner taps my thigh, indicating for me to jump up so we can grab our food. I do, and we head over to the small fold out table where Connor and Ross have laid out all the food. I grab a hot dog and a burger before scooping up some potato salad we bought from the small shop earlier. I wait until Banner finishes filling his plate before heading back to our chair.

"You sit there," he tells me. "I'm gonna sit on the log to eat this, and then we can go for our walk."

"You can't sit on that; it's cold," I protest. "You'll get piles."

He laughs at my horrified expression. "Just eat your food."

"No, I'll sit on your lap like before."

He shakes his head, sitting down on the log. "Just sit down and eat your food, Emma. I promise, my arse will be fine. But, I'm glad you're looking out for it."

When he winks, I blush, mumbling, "Oh, all right then."

It doesn't take us long to finish our food. Banner grabs us some torches from the tent before coming back for me, handing me one.

"Guys, can you keep some water boiled for when we get back? We want to make some hot chocolate before we go to bed," he tells the lads.

"You have hot chocolate?" Kelsea asks, licking her lips.

"Only two sachets," Banner lies, not looking at her. I look away, so she can't see my smile. We still have half a box and a massive pack of marshmallows.

He takes my hand and we head towards the path leading into the forest.

"Don't let any bugs bite you on the arse," Tom yells, before laughing.

"And don't fuck up a tree. You'll get splinters," Connor shouts.

"Connor, you said you wouldn't tell anyone," Kelsea hisses.

Everyone laughs around the campfire, and I can't stop my own from spilling free.

"Fuckers!" Banner groans. "We're going for a walk to get away from you sad fucks."

"Keep telling yourself that," Rafner shouts.

We both turn to see him spanking mid-air, thrusting his hips. I giggle, shaking my head.

Banner squeezes my hand, pulling me towards the entrance of the forest. A cold shiver runs down my spine, as I feel eyes on me. I look around, not seeing anything, and only hearing the noises from the lads in the background.

I shine my torch on the ground to light up the path, not wanting to get lost.

"It's kind of creepy in here," I whisper, looking around the darkened forest.

He laughs, pulling me close. "Sorry, but I wanted to get you alone for a bit. I think Tom and Connor have a crush."

I giggle. The two are always flirting with me, but it's just banter. "They're harmless."

"They'll be armless if they keep on," he mutters. "How are you feeling? Are your ribs still hurting you? I'm sorry about the sleeping conditions—I didn't even think."

I squeeze his hand. "Banner, it's fine. They ached for all of an hour. I can deal with that." Sleeping on an air mattress wasn't the best idea for my ribs. I woke up stiff and sore. It was the first time for a few weeks that I had to take something for the pain.

He stops us by the edge of the river. The slope leading down looks steep, and I shiver, stepping back. It looks angry, running fast and smacking up the side of the bank as it flows downstream.

He grips my chin softly, turning my head so we're facing. The breath I was about to take freezes in my lungs at the look in his eyes.

"There's something I've wanted to tell you for a while," his whispers, his voice husky.

"There is?" I ask breathlessly.

His thumb caresses my jawline, and my eyes droop as my body sways forward.

"Yeah."

"What is it?" I ask, moving closer. If I didn't know any better, I'd say he was nervous. But that can't be right. He never gets nervous.

"Emma, I—"

He pauses in confusion when my eyes go round with fear. Stepping up behind him is dark figure, and I know in my gut this isn't one of the lads playing around. Before I can scream and warn him, something swings in the air. Seeing my expression, he looks over his shoulder, but it's too late. He turns back to me, his eyes wide with horror. I cringe at the sound of the branch hitting him, the sickening crunch turning my stomach. He tries to reach for me at the same time I reach for him, but the man stalking me hits him one more time. Our fingers slide against each other's, and I scream when he falls backwards, down the bank, splashing into the water.

"Banner!" I scream, moving to take a step towards the river, needing to get to him. He's going to freeze to death, and that's only if he's conscious. If he's not, he could drown.

A hand grabs my arm, swinging me around and smacking me in the face. I cry out, taking a few steps back, getting ready to run. My torch drops to the ground.

I need to get to Banner.

Terrified, I glance at our attacker, my eyes widening when they step into the light. "Mr. Flint."

"Did you think I would have forgotten you, you silly fucking cow."

I look to the river, not seeing Banner anymore. I rub my chest, feeling tears flowing down my cheeks. I may have just lost the one man I could ever truly, deeply love. He's my one and only, and I never got to tell him how I feel.

From the corner of my eye, Mr. Flint jumps forward, grabbing me by my coat when I move back too quickly. He looks rough, like he's been in the wars, and the stench coming from him is overwhelming.

"Get off me," I scream, hoping someone from the camp can hear me.

With strength I didn't know anyone could possess, he throws me, and I land with a thud against a tree, sliding down.

"I'm going to fuck you, then fucking kill you, you snivelling, whiny little whore." He laughs humorously. "And to think I thought you were meek and weak."

I watch in horror as he pulls out a silver knife, the moon reflecting off the large, sharpened blade. I yelp, fear churning in my stomach when he steps closer. Quickly, I shuffle to my feet, my back pressed against the tree, holding my hands out in front of me.

"Please don't," I cry out, my life flashing before my eyes. For a long time, I had nothing to live for. I had nothing I *wanted* to live for. I had lost everything, and I was drowning in depression. Then Banner climbed in through my bedroom window, the same night I took an overdose, and made everything easier. Day by day, he made me feel alive again.

I have people in my life now who I love and adore. God wouldn't take Banner from me, not after he gave him to me. And for him, I need to get through this. He needs me. He could be struggling in that river, calling out for help, and I'm stuck here with a lunatic.

"There's no one here to save you this time, Emma. Your boyfriend's dead." He laughs, sounding crazed. "When I get done with you, I'm going to cut your insides out. You'll be screaming for help and no one will hear you. No one is going to save you." He holds the knife up, a murderous glint in his eye. "The only option you have left is whether you make this easier on yourself. Not that I mind you fighting, just expect the pain that is to follow."

I scan the empty forest, seeing no one or nothing that can help me, deflating any hope I had of surviving this. There is not a weapon in sight, nothing to help get me away from him. I could try to run, but the size of the forest… I'd be lost before I got far, and that's if he doesn't catch me first.

I hear him go for me, and I close my eyes, waiting for the blow I know is about to happen. Only, instead, I hear a scuffle. My eyes fly open with hope.

Banner.

But it's not him.

I'm confused when I see Darren standing there, panting, holding a thick, fallen branch in his hand.

"Get the fuck away now. I've called the police," Darren growls, standing between me and Mr. Flint.

Mr. Flint clutches his stomach, looking winded. "Who the fuck are you—another one she's fucking?"

I shrink back against the tree at the venomous look he gives me. Darren steps to the side, blocking him from seeing me.

"I'm your worst fucking nightmare. Now step back."

I scream when Mr. Flint jumps forward, holding the knife out in front of him. Darren goes back on one leg, bracing for the attack. Everything happens so quickly.

I glance to the river where Banner fell, but I'm torn when I hear a grunt of pain. I look back just as Mr. Flint bends at the waist, before tackling Darren, sending them both flying to the floor.

I look around for a weapon, crying with frustration when I don't see anything.

Darren howls in agony, and the sound runs through my soul. I flinch at the punch he lands on Mr. Flint's jaw, knocking him backwards to the floor. The knife falls to the ground and I rush over, grabbing it and throwing it as far into the forest as I can manage.

When I turn back around, Darren has the branch in his hand again, hitting a dazed Mr. Flint around the head. His eyes roll back, and I jump when Darren hits him again, not satisfied until he's fallen to the floor with a sickening thud.

"Darren?" I call when he wobbles backwards, looking at me with wide eyes. He drops the branch, clutching his stomach.

"You need to find Banner. He's on the bank—just down a bit," he gasps out, falling to his knees.

"He's okay?" I ask in relief as I rush over to the torch.

"He's not conscious, but I managed to pull him out of the water," he chokes out. I pick up the torch and turn around to shine it on Darren, ready to ask him what he's doing here. It's not that I'm not grateful—he's just saved mine and Banner's lives.

The light illuminates Darren's body, and a loud gasp escapes me. I feel the blood drain from my face when I see the rips in his shirt, blood oozing down his chest.

Oh, my God.

"Oh, my God, did he stab you?" I ask, rushing over.

He falls backwards on his back, staring up at the sky. "So, this is karma," he gasps, coughing up blood.

I put the torch on his stomach, shining it on his stab wounds, and force the bile down that threatens to rise. I take off my gloves, pressing them into the wound, and apply pressure. I scan the deserted forest, panicked when the gloves don't stop the flow of blood, the warm fluid running through my fingers. "Help—somebody help," I scream, tears falling down my cheeks.

Darren places his hand on top of mine, cringing in pain.

"Go. Go make sure Banner is okay."

"I'm not leaving you, not like this," I tell him as my throat tightens.

"Who would have thought you would be helping me after all I did." He moans, his back arching as he tries to get comfortable. "I'm sorry. I'm sorry for everything."

I shake my head at him, pressing harder on his wounds. "No! Not like this. We need to get you to the hospital, and then, when you're better—you can tell me then. It's going to be okay."

"I need—I need to explain. I—"

"Please, you don't need to do this. Let's concentrate on getting you help." Blinking through tears, I lift my head and scream, "Help! Somebody help me!"

"I didn't—I wasn't… I wasn't going to rape you. You have to know that," he says, struggling to get his words out.

"I know you wasn't," I cry, a sob breaking through. "I was never sure because it was a blur, but after Mr. Flint attacked me, I know that was never your intention."

"I loved your sister, Emma. I just loved Lake more. When your sister kept doing more drugs, I chose Lake. I never wanted her to hurt. It's why I started taking them, to ease the pain."

"Why did you sell her those drugs?" I blurt out, watching his pale face close off in pain.

"She would have gone anywhere to get them, done anything to get her next fix. When I ran out, I didn't want her to get in trouble by going elsewhere. There are dickheads around who would have used her. I got some from another dealer, so she wouldn't have to. I didn't know they were laced with poison. I swear, I didn't." He starts choking again, and I feel like I can't breathe, watching him turn paler by the second.

"Please don't die. Please."

"I'm so sorry," he cries, tears falling down his cheeks.

"*I'm* sorry," I cry, trying to stop the bleeding. "What were you doing here, anyway."

"That day at the university, I saw someone hiding behind the bushes after you left. They didn't think I noticed, but I did. I saw him go into the university, so I waited for the class to finish before following him to an old farm house. When nothing happened, I left."

He starts coughing, clutching his stomach. "You didn't want to see me again, and I understood, so I never did anything. I didn't even think any more of it until I saw his face in the paper. I knew it was you he attacked. I've gone back to the farmhouse every night for the past two weeks, and then yesterday morning, he left, following you guys up here. I've been watching him watch you. I wanted to come out and warn you, but I didn't want to get in a fight."

"So, you decided to save me instead?"

"You didn't deserve what happened to you, Emma. What I did to you, and then what he did. I was a messed-up kid. So yes, I helped you." He wheezes, clutching his chest. When blood starts pouring from the corner of his mouth, I begin to panic.

"Somebody, please, help me," I scream, my voice echoing off the trees.

"Emma?"

"Tom, I'm over here," I scream, before looking down at Darren. "Hold on, Darren, help is here."

"I'm sorry," he gasps, his eyes rolling to the back of his head.

"No, Darren, stay awake," I cry.

"Emma!"

"Sorry," Darren whispers. "I'm so sorry."

"I forgive you. Darren, can you hear me? I forgive you."

His eyes barely open, a small smile playing on his lips, before his entire body just collapses, one last breath expelling from his lungs before… nothing. He just lies there, not moving a muscle.

"Darren, no!" I wail, pressing down on his chest. I shake him, but his head just flops to the side, lifeless.

I scream, sobs racking through my chest, clutching what is left of his shirt in my hands. I place a hand on his cheek, stroking him softly. "Please, wake up. Please. I forgive you," I shout, crying harder.

Footsteps come bursting through the bushes, but I can't look away from Darren, my head falling against his chest.

"What the fuck? Emma?" Tom yells, rushing over to me, lifting me off Darren. I can feel his blood all over me as I look helplessly at Tom.

"What the fuck happened?" Connor shouts, looking around at the two dead bodies. "Oh, fuck. Isn't that the English teacher?"

Tom shakes me, and I look up at him, feeling numb. "Emma, where's Banner?"

"Mr. Flint hit him, and he fell into the river," I choke out, feeling my chest tighten with pain.

"Oh, fuck," Connor hisses, placing his hands on his head. "It's fucking freezing."

Tears gather behind Tom's eyes. "Was he alive?"

Fat tears slide down my cheeks as I look down at Darren. "He said Banner was just down by the river bank. He pulled him out. He saved him," I whisper.

"Go look, Connor," Tom yells, pulling out his phone. I listen to him call for an ambulance, just as more people come through the trees. "Guys, stay back. Don't let any of the girls here."

"What's going on?" Rafner asks, and I feel him move closer. "Holy fucking shit."

"I've called an ambulance and they said the police are on their way too. Can you go tell one of the girls that they need to wait by the tree-line for them—and one of them at the entrance, so they know where to go?"

"Yeah, be right back," he says, sounding shocked.

I still don't look away from Darren, feeling lost.

"Bro, I need help," Connor yells. I look up, finding him struggling with Banner. He's not moving, his chin dropped to his chest.

"Banner," I cry out, rushing to my feet. I help try to support him as we lie him down near Darren. I take in his appearance, my heart breaking in two. He has a gash on the side of his head, blooding seeping down his face, and his lips are blue.

Connor takes his coat off, placing it over Banner. Tom does the same, coming to sit next to me as I begin to shake.

"What happened, Emma?"

"Mr. Flint… he came out of nowhere, Tom. He hit Banner with a branch, and he went into the water. Then he pulled a knife on me. He was going to stab me—*rape* me," I whisper. "Then Darren tackled him.

I don't know—it happened so fast. Darren hit him with the branch, and I thought it was over. There was so much blood," I whisper, looking down at my hands, which are still covered in Darren's blood. I start sobbing, trying to wipe it off on my coat.

"Get it off me," I scream, wiping more furiously. It's still there, staining my skin and soul.

"Shh, it's okay. I got you," Tom soothes, placing his hands over mine.

"Please, get it off me," I whisper, feeling dizzy.

"Who's Darren?" Connor asks, and I feel Tom stiffen next to me.

I let out a dry laugh, wiping my eyes with the sleeve of my coat. "He's the lad who attacked me a few years ago and put me in hospital."

"Um, what the fuck!"

"Bro, just drop it," Tom says softly, but his voice holds warning.

"Okay."

"The ambulance is here," Rafner breathes out, gasping for air as he runs back into the clearing. He looks as pale as the rest of us, staring down at the two lifeless bodies.

Two paramedics come rushing through the trees, their lights bright, making me blink, wincing. I fall against Tom, watching blankly as one works on Banner while the other announces the other two dead.

It's then that the night's events catch up to me and I pass out, my head feeling heavy.

Chapter 20

The paramedics are pushing me through A&E when I hear a commotion close by. I jump, startled at the noise. I close my eyes, rejecting the sound, and the voices fade into the background.

"It's okay, Emma," Tom says, taking my hand as they wheel me into a room. A sudden chill sweeps through me and I begin to shake uncontrollably. My pulse races as I stare, in a daze, at Tom.

Tom grabs the blanket from the bottom of the bed, pulling it over me. I watch him, feeling detached from my body.

He looks over his shoulder, his lips moving as he talks to someone. I blink, feeling numb. He steps aside and, in his place, Mark and Levi stand in front of me, bending down so we're eye level.

Marks lips move, but I can barely make them out. It sounds like I'm swimming under water. "Emma, baby, are you okay?"

I blink.

Mark is talking to Tom, running a frustrated hand through his hair, making it stick up. I want to tell him to straighten it before a male nurse walks in, but nothing comes out.

I blink.

Levi holds Mark, rubbing his hands up and down his back as Mark's shoulders shake.

I roll away from them, facing the other side of the small cubicle they put me in. A nurse comes to check the IV the paramedic put in me, before pressing buttons on a machine.

I barely feel the tightness around my arm, too paralysed to even investigate what it is. My eyes close tightly, shutting everything and everyone around me out.

∽

"Have they said what's wrong with her?"

"She's in shock. She's not processing. It's bad, Banner. They're talking about admitting her into the psych ward," Mark says, his voice gruff.

"Banner, you need to go rest. You've got a concussion and a head injury," Levi demands. "If her condition changes, I'll come and find you."

"I'm not leaving her," Banner growls, his voice husky and dry.

"Mate, we can watch her," Mark says, agreeing with Levi.

"I said fucking no," Banner snaps. The sound has me jumping, opening my eyes. "Emma?"

I blink over at Banner, tears gathering in my eyes when I see the bandage wrapped around his head. He runs a finger down the side of my face, forcing a small smile.

"Banner?" I croak, my throat raw.

"Emma? Oh, my God, you're awake. Are you okay? Do you need anything? Should we get a nurse?" Mark rushes out, coming around the bed to stand next to Banner. Levi comes into view next and I blink back more tears, feeling my throat tighten. I glance back at Banner, needing to touch him, to make sure he's real. I can't move though, too afraid it's an illusion. "There was so much blood, Banner. So much."

I close my eyes when I'm bombarded with images of the night's events. I keep seeing Darren's face, the anguish and pain written all over it. I know he tried to hold back, not wanting to show me just how badly he hurt. But I could read it in his eyes.

I close my eyes tighter when I see the moment Banner fell into the river, the torment I saw there. He looked petrified, but not for himself—for me.

"I'm sorry, Emma. So sorry," Banner whispers.

I blink my eyes open, letting the tears I was afraid to let fall, flow down my cheeks. "I thought I lost you forever when you fell into that river." As soon as the words escape my lips, I break down, sobbing into the pillow. I clutch it in a tight grasp, the pain in my chest unbearable.

I'm moved, and then Banner's climbing into bed with me and laying me on his chest. "Shh, baby, I got you. You're safe now."

As I cry harder into his chest, I feel Mark or Levi, or both, place their hands on my legs, squeezing them gently in a soothing gesture, showing they are here for me.

"Darren saved me. He died saving me," I sob. "I tried to help him, but he died in my arms. He died."

At a loss for words, Banner doesn't say anything. He holds me closer, running his fingers through my knotted hair.

I press closer to him, feeling my tears soak his hospital gown. I begin to feel drowsy, and I struggle to keep my eyes open through my tears.

"Go to sleep, Emma."

"Don't leave me," I whisper.

"Never," he vows, kissing the top of my head.

⁓

I'm groggy when I wake, feeling a hard chest beneath me. I glance up, seeing Banner's handsome face in a deep sleep. He's no longer wearing the bandage, and instead, has a plaster covering where he got bashed in the head. A bruise runs down the side of his face. As I run my gaze down the rest of his body, I make out scratches on his neck, a few bruises, and more on his arms.

He got so lucky. I really could have lost him.

I look down the bed into my room, jumping when I find Mark watching me, Levi asleep next to him in a chair. I wasn't expecting him to still be here.

"Mark?" I call out, seeing the tortured expression on his face. He gets up from his chair in the corner, moving to sit down in the one next to the bed. His eyes water as he reaches out to take my hand from Banner's chest, clutching it in his.

"When I got the phone call a week ago, I thought I lost you," he chokes out, his eyes closing with despair.

"Wait! A week ago?"

He opens his eyes at my question, nodding. "Yeah. You only woke up yesterday, Emma. You've been in and out of it all week. You've not spoken to anyone."

I feel tears gather behind my eyes. "I'm so sorry," I tell him, only imagining how scared he must have been.

"Never scare me like that again. I had to fight your mum and dad over medical guardianship over you."

"What?" I wince at how loud I'm being, feeling Banner stir beneath me.

"Is everything okay?" he asks.

Mark looks up at him, his eyes telling him everything. "I was just telling Emma her parents have been here." My heart picks up, hoping they came to see how I was, but the look Mark gives me deflates any hope. "I had our grandparents come down. They tried to get you committed into a psych ward after the doctors recommended it. Since you weren't able to make any medical decisions, they had to call them."

I look at the poster behind his head. "Thank you for not letting them," I whisper.

"It's the least I could do. Emma, please, never go off in that head of yours again. I thought we lost you. It was like you weren't in your own body."

A tear falls.

"I'm sorry."

He squeezes my hand, letting me go. "Don't be, baby. I'm so fucking glad you're okay."

"Am I okay?"

He nods, puzzled at my question. "Yes—apart from a few bruises, there was nothing physically wrong with you. They said you went into a mental state of shock and shut down. It's a way for your mind to protect you from what happened."

"I still can't believe it happened."

"I didn't see him coming," Banner whispers. "I couldn't even help you."

I look up at the sound of anguish in his voice. "You couldn't have known he was there. I didn't even get a chance to warn you. I froze, and then everything happened so quickly."

"What happened after I fell into the water?"

I close my eyes at the memories, still feeling Mr. Flint's hands on my biceps. When I open them, Mark sits forward, listening intently.

"He hit me, threw me into a tree, and said what he was going to do to me. I was going to fight, not let him win, but I believed what he said. When I couldn't find a weapon, I gave up. I just gave up. I prepared myself to be killed—to die," I croak out.

Banner squeezes me tighter. "You don't have to do this if you don't want to."

"I remember closing my eyes, thinking of you guys, already missing you, when I heard a scuffle. I couldn't believe Darren was there, or that he stood in between me and Mr. Flint. He protected me from the beginning. I didn't even know he had been stabbed, Banner. I watched as he bashed Mr. Flint over the head with so much strength I heard the impact. It was horrifying. Blood just poured from him, but I didn't care. I was just happy he was dead."

"And Darren?" Mark whispers.

"I shined the light on him, and he was bleeding from two wounds in his chest. I tried to help him. He said he followed Mr. Flint to us. Apparently, he saw him watching me from the trees at the university the day he came to talk to me. If it wasn't for Darren, I'd be dead. Mr. Flint planned to rape me before he killed me, Banner." I begin to cry, hiding my face in his chest.

"He died a hero, baby," Banner whispers.

"He found redemption in death. Something he was probably looking for, for a long time," Mark adds.

"I told him I forgave him," I admit through sobs. "And I did. I forgave him, because the person I saw dying in my arms… he wasn't the same person who attacked me all those years ago. Do you think he heard me?"

"Yes, baby, I do."

It's then I notice my arm. "Is that a new cast?"

Mark nods. "Yours was broken. You must have landed on it and didn't feel it from the shock. They gave you another x-ray and found another fracture—only mild—then recast it. Does it hurt?"

"No," I whisper, blinking at the pale cast. "I don't remember them doing it."

Someone raps on the door and I glance down the bed, seeing Levi is awake and listening. He gives me a soft smile before turning to the person at the door.

"You're awake," Tom announces, surprised. In his hands are a jar of flowers and some chocolates.

"Hey, bro," Connor announces, holding a teddy and a balloon.

"What are you doing here?" Banner asks, sounding as surprised as I am to see them.

Connor gives him a dirty look before coming to sit on the empty chair Mark left. "Not to see your ugly mug, that's for sure."

"So, the flowers aren't for me?" Banner teases.

He helps me sit up as we face the group of people. Tom comes to the other side of the bed, placing the items he has on the cabinet.

"I bought these for you. I didn't think you were awake. When we checked yesterday, they said you were still out of it."

"Thank you." I share a look with him, one of understanding. He witnessed what I did, saw the aftermath of what Mr. Flint caused. "For everything," I tell him, with a deeper meaning.

He gives me a small smile. "Glad you're doing okay. You had me worried. They wouldn't let us stay with you once your cousins got here. They only let us in at visiting times."

"Whose friend are you?" Banner asks, not sounding mad but amused.

"Sorry, dude, but your girl has us for life. She's a fucking rock star."

I giggle, cuddling closer to Banner. "I wouldn't go that far."

Tom's expression turns serious. "I would. I didn't witness what you went through, but I did see the aftermath, and it was fucking deadly."

"Bro, wrong choice of words," Connor groans.

Tom winces, giving me an apologetic look. "Sorry."

"It's fine," I whisper.

"What I meant is, you stayed strong until you knew Banner was safe. You kept it mostly together. You're one strong chick."

I don't answer, not feeling very strong right now. My stomach chooses that moment to announce to the room it's hungry.

Everyone stares at my belly with wide eyes before laughing. Levi gets up, straightening out his clothes.

"I'll go down the road to the pizza place. The food here is fucking disgusting."

My stomach growls again. I shrug, feeling my cheeks heat. "Sounds good."

Banner starts chatting to his friends, asking what he missed and what has happened. I tune them out, only needing the warmth and safety of Banner's presence.

After nearly losing him, I know there is no way I can ever sit back and watch him be with someone else. It's time for me to take a stand, to show him I can be strong, that I'm ready to love him.

He's not going to know what hit him. By the time I'm done, he's going to know how I really feel about him.

A life without him isn't a life worth living. I learnt that lesson in the forest.

But for now, I need to recover. Waiting a few days, after the years I've spent secretly loving him, won't hurt.

Chapter 21

My palms are sweaty as I sit waiting for our guest to arrive, so I wipe them down my jeans. My leg bounces, my entire body on edge.

After I was released a few days ago, we had a phone call from my solicitor, asking if Darren's aunt could come see me. I readily agreed, especially after he saved my life. But the second I got off the phone, doubt crept in.

What if she blames me for his death?

What if she wants revenge or justice?

The thoughts kept running through my mind.

The only saving grace was Becky. She finally found the courage to leave her house and come visit me the day I was released from hospital. We spoke about everything. She felt terrible for everything, even pushing me away after the attack at the university. But after a long talk, I managed to convince her to forgive herself and not to worry. We were friends, nothing was going to change that.

"Will you stop bouncing your leg, it's making me nervous," Banner orders from next to me.

I grimace, giving him an apologetic smile. "Sorry. I'm just really nervous. What if she's come to tell me she hates me, Banner?"

"Then I'll kick her fucking arse."

"And I'll throw the bitch out," Mark pipes in from the kitchen doorway.

When there's a knock on the door, I practically jump out of my seat.

"Calm down. I'll get it," Banner tells me, getting up from the sofa and walking over to the door.

"I'll go to my room," Mark whispers, rushing over to his room.

I watch, my fingers twiddling in my lap. Banner opens the door to reveal a petite woman with mousy brown hair and kind eyes.

"Hey, I'm Diana. Darren's aunt."

"Come in," Banner tells her curtly.

She looks nervous, looking around the room warily like someone's going to jump out at her. When her eyes land on me on the couch, tears gather behind them.

"You must be Emma," she says softly.

I quickly stand, nodding. "Yes. Please, have a seat."

"I can't stay long. I have to pick the kids up from nursery."

"Okay."

She sits down elegantly, crossing her legs to the side and folding her hands in her lap. "As you're aware, Darren came to live with me after he was released from prison. His mum wasn't the best, and his father left and never looked back when he was three. She never showed him the love or attention a child deserved, even a teenager who should be getting reprimanded for being in trouble. She didn't care."

"Why are you telling me this?" I ask quietly.

She gives me a sad smile, tilting her head to the side. "To show you what kind of person he was. His mum turned to drugs, and to feed her habit, she had him sell drugs for her dealer. I tried to intervene at that point, but he loved his mum. He just wanted her to change, to love him. One of her boyfriends got violent, and when his mum still didn't leave him, Darren changed.

"I visited him in prison, since his mum no longer cared. She had forgotten about him. It took him a long time to get through withdrawal, but once he did, that boy broke before my very eyes. He told me everything. He told me about loving your sister, but that she reminded him too much of his mum. He also loved his girlfriend more—at the time. He said she was a breath of fresh air, an escape from the reality of his life and what it had become. I got a phone call the same day, saying he'd tried to hang himself in his cell."

I gasp, feeling tears gather in my eyes. I didn't know any of this. I didn't even know about his mum, and thinking back, I can't remember ever meeting her.

"When he attacked you, he didn't even realise what he was doing. It's no excuse, and he took full responsibility, but he wanted an escape from the life he was leading. He watched his mum doing it his whole life and thought that was the answer," she says, wiping away the tears falling down her cheeks.

"You don't need to do this," I tell her, my chest tightening.

"He would want me to. I *need* to," she explains. "He never got over attacking you, even with the counselling the prison provided. He tried to write to you a few times, wanting you to know how deeply sorry he was. When he was given a release date, I provided everything, even a job for him to come out to. But you haunted him night and day. He would scream out your name at night," she says, clutching her chest, her voice hitching.

Banner sits down next to me, wrapping his arm around my chest. "I'm so sorry, Diana."

She looks up, surprise in her eyes. "Never be sorry, Emma. What he did was unforgivable, but it still didn't mean he couldn't make amends."

"I did forgive him. For everything," I whisper.

She starts shaking with sobs, taking a tissue out of her bag to blow her nose. I remain quiet, letting her have her moment.

"You did?"

I give her a soft smile. "I did. He saved my life, Diana. What he did was brave and courageous. He stood in front of a knife for me," I choke out. "I thought you had come to blame me today, to tell me you hated me for being responsible for his death."

"Oh, you sweet girl. You aren't responsible any more than I am. He would have wanted this. All he wanted was to make amends. I'm going to miss my nephew terribly. Underneath all that arrogance and bad boy persona, he was a good boy. He felt deeply—too deeply. And all he wanted in this world was for you to forgive him."

I lean against Banner, my heart hurting. "I'm sorry he died, and for your loss."

"Thank you, Emma. That's means the world coming from you."

"You're welcome."

"That's all I wanted to say. I couldn't move forward until I finished what he what he wanted to accomplish. Thank you so much for taking the time to listen to me."

I stand when she does, stepping forward and pulling her in for a hug. "Thank you for coming. And I'm sorry again. So sorry," I say into her shoulder.

She hugs me tighter before pulling away, her watery smile making my chin wobble.

"Live a happy life, Emma."

"You too," I force through the lump in my throat.

We walk her to the door, saying one last goodbye before quietly shutting it behind her.

I turn to Banner once she's left, not knowing what to say. "Didn't expect that," he whispers, pulling me closer, his hands on my hips.

"Me neither," I admit, tilting my neck up to see him.

"You doing okay?"

I shrug, not knowing how to feel. "I'm feeling a lot right now."

He runs his finger down my cheek, something he does often. "Emma, I love you."

I raise an eyebrow. "I love you too."

He smirks, shaking his head. He leans closer, his lips brushing mine, and I gasp. His thick, dark eyelashes brush across my cheeks. "Emma, you're not hearing me. I'm in love with you."

"Has she gone?" Mark blurts out, stepping out of his room.

Banner pulls away, glaring at Mark. "Can't a guy kiss his fucking girl without being interrupted?"

"Huh?" Mark mutters, looking to each of us for answers.

"Fuck this," Banner curses, before grabbing me.

I don't have time to prepare before his lips are on mine in a punishing kiss. He dips me a little, pressing me against him. I moan into his mouth, opening a little to give him access.

I never thought it would feel this good.

Another moan escapes me, and I clutch his T-shirt tighter in my fingers, needing to be closer.

His tongue does another sweep, and I feel like I could pass out from the ecstasy.

When he pulls away, his face still close, I'm breathing heavily, staring up at him with stars in my eyes.

"Wow," I breathe out.

He grins, kissing me once more. "I love you, Emma. I've loved you for a long time. You just never noticed me with Lake around."

"Lake?" I ask, wondering what she has to do with this.

"Emma, I've loved you since you were twelve years old and I saw you picking up litter in the park. You looked so beautiful, even covered in dirt and grime."

"Since I was twelve?" I ask, stunned. I remember that time in my life. I went through a faze where I made everyone on our street recycle, and I made my grandparents buy me a litter picker. I wanted to make a difference.

He nods, rubbing his hands up my sides. "Yeah."

I soften further against him, feeling the love seep through my veins. "I love you too, Banner. I've not loved you as long, but I can tell you I love you just as much."

His expressions soften, his eyes shining back at me. "I didn't have the courage to do this when you were twelve, and I don't have a love note with tick yes or no boxes, but I have to ask. Will you, Emma Burton, be my girlfriend?"

I laugh, nodding. He swings me around, his face lit up with happiness, before he drops me to my feet.

His lips reach mine, kissing me deeply and thoroughly.

This… this I could get used to.

I could spend the rest of my life kissing him, loving him. And he doesn't know it yet, but I plan to make him happy for the rest of his life.

Because one day, I am going to marry him.

Epilogue

Ten Years Later

I knew that one day this day would come. I dreamt of it for so long. I just didn't anticipate how nervous I would be.

I bend down when little hands pull on my dress and look at the beautiful little girl with her chubby cheeks and bright, round, blue eyes.

"Lily-Mae, you look like a princess," I tell her, truly blessed to have her in my life.

"Where are my daddies?" she whispers, looking around with curious eyes. "I might need a poo-poo soon."

I laugh at her bluntness, hugging my niece. Technically, she's my second cousin, but when Mark and Levi adopted her four years ago, I couldn't picture being anything other than her auntie.

"Lily-Mae, your daddies are waiting for you at the end of the aisle, waiting to see you in your beautiful dress."

She huffs, her chubby cheeks blowing up before she inhales, crossing her arms over her chest. "We'd better get this show on da road den."

She never fails to bring a smile to my face. "Yep. I have my Prince Charming waiting for me at the end of the aisle."

And I do. The past ten years have been a whirlwind. I've loved him harder and stronger with each day that's passed. We've had to make some adjustments along the way, but we've pulled through. There is nothing that could tear us apart.

Her adorable little face scrunches up in disgust. "Uncle Banner eats all da best ice cream. He no Princes Charming."

I giggle when she begins to pout. "I promise to hide some extra ice cream, just for you."

Her entire face lights up and my heart squeezes in my chest. "You are da best auntie ever."

Even though her words make me happy, it still makes me sad that she's missing out on the aunties and uncles she could have had through Mark's siblings. None of them have gotten in touch with him since he left home. It's like they were hoping he'd all of a sudden be into girls. Now he's married, has a beautiful daughter, and is going the adoption route again.

I stand up straight, waiting for Jordan to take the little girl's hand. "You look beautiful," she tells me.

I reach over and squeeze her hand. "Thank you. You look beautiful too. Thank you again for wearing a dress."

She glares teasingly at me. "I wouldn't do this for anyone else."

She totally would. She's a big softie under all those piercings and tattoos.

"I'm so freaking emotional right now, I could cry," Becky blurts out, before bursting into tears.

I begin to laugh at my heavily pregnant friend. "Becky, don't cry. You'll ruin your makeup."

She waves a tissue in the air. "I'm going to kill Connor for knocking me up. I'll wait until after the wedding, though," she tells me.

"I'm grateful," I tease.

Lake comes rushing around the corner, looking stressed and out of breath. "I'm so sorry. The triplets got into the food next door. I had to chase Hayden and Landon whilst Max tried to get Liam down."

"Down from where?"

To this very day, I still can't believe my best friend had triplets. Max didn't do things by half, that's for sure. He had a ring on her finger a year after she came back into my life, and they married the year after that. When she told me she was pregnant, I wasn't surprised. It was only when she announced she was expecting triplets that I thought she was playing a prank on me.

Now, she has three boisterous kids. Hayden, the only girl, being the worst out of the three. Sometimes I think she controls the boys, but her sweet, innocent little face will have you believing otherwise. They are always up to something or getting into trouble.

"He climbed up the scaffolding where the lights are. It's fine—Max got them down and has them sitting down in the hall now." Becky helps Lake straighten her hair before Jordan passes her a bouquet of flowers. "Right, let's do this before Banner thinks you've run away and comes out to chase you."

I give them a bright smile, taking my granddad's arm. He kisses me on the cheek, looking down at me with watery eyes.

"You look so beautiful, just like your nan did on her wedding day," he tells me, sounding choked up.

We lost my nan three years ago to a heart attack. My granddad hasn't been the same since. And I can understand; I hope, when the day comes, I will be gone before Banner. I don't think I'd survive the heartache of losing him, and I wouldn't want to.

"I love you," I tell him, leaning my head on his shoulder briefly before straightening.

The bridesmaids go first, the wedding march playing softly in the background. I wanted to go the traditional route, not some new pop love song they play on the radio. I wanted everything: the church, the wedding march, and the throwing of the bouquet. And although I may not get my father-daughter dance, I will get my granddad, and he means more to me than my parents, who I haven't spoken to since I left home.

I inhale when it's our turn and take my first step to the next part of my life.

Tears gather in my eyes when they land on Banner standing at the end of the aisle. He was standing straight, holding his hands behind his back, but the second he sees me, his hands fall to his sides and his jaw drops.

He takes a step forward, making me smile. Mark, one of his many groomsmen, pulls him back by the bottom of suit jacket.

He doesn't pay attention, his gaze only for me. The sea of faces surrounding us blur into each other, because I can't take my eyes off him. I know they're there; I can feel their gazes on me. I just don't care to look, or to be polite, not when everything I could ever want is standing right in front of me.

"Who gives this woman?" the priest asks.

"I do!" Granddad says, bringing a lump to my throat, just like it did the night before at our rehearsal.

"I do," Mark suddenly says, shocking me. That wasn't meant to be said by him. I fight hard not to cry at the pride shining in his eyes.

"I do," Levi speaks up, stepping forward also.

"I do," Tom says, and I begin to choke up. Since that night in the woods, we've become best friends. It was the same way with Connor, but with Tom… we share a bond. He held me in my darkest moments, and I'll never forget that.

When no one else speaks up, I let a tear fall, praying it hasn't ruined my makeup. Granddad places my hand in Banner's, leaning down to kiss me on my cheek. The others follow, placing their own kisses on my cheek before taking their places.

I squeeze Banner's hand, ready to start a new chapter in our lives, knowing this is the best decision I ever made.

∼

Ed Sheeran's *Perfect* starts playing as Banner takes my hand and pulls me onto the dance floor. I laugh when he swings me out before pulling me towards him, his free hand going to my hip.

"I love you, Mrs. Banner."

My cheeks hurt so badly from smiling so much. I didn't think I could ever feel so happy, but I do. I'm so blissfully happy I could burst.

"I love you too, husband."

He smirks down at me. "I like the sound of that."

"Me too."

I wrap my arms around his neck, his hands falling down to my hips as we sway to the music. Today couldn't have gone more perfect.

And Banner's vows… I can feel my throat closing up as I remember them.

"I'm so lucky to have met you, and today, I get to marry my best friend, my soul mate. I get to share my life with you. I get to build a future with you.

"Today, I promise to love you unconditionally; to listen respectfully when

you get mad; hold you when you get sad; and make you laugh every day. I will treasure each moment we share, knowing forever will never be enough.

"Emma Burton, you have been my best friend, my girlfriend, and my fiancé. Today, I make you my wife, but no matter the title, you'll always be each of those things to me. My love, my dream, my devotion. You, Emma, are my everything. I love you."

A small body slams into my legs, snapping me out of my daydream. I look down at Hayden, who looks up with a sheepish expression.

"Sorry," Hayden whisper-yells. "Don't tell Mummy."

I giggle when she runs away, her brothers not far behind her. I glance back at my husband, holding him tighter.

"Hey, this is meant to be a happy day," he says when he sees my watery eyes.

"I'm just so happy."

His smile is soft as he squeezes my hip. "It couldn't have gone better. You've made me the happiest man."

"Oh, I don't know about that," I tell him evasively.

He raises a brow. "What do you mean?"

"It could get better," I tell him, running my finger down his chest, above where I know my name is inked.

He waggles his eyebrows. "Oh yeah, what did you have in mind?"

I giggle at his expression, then blink up at him through my lashes before leaning up on my tip toes, my lips brushing his ear. "I'm pregnant."

He pulls back, scanning my face to see if I'm joking. Seeing the truth, he grins big before lifting me up in the air and spinning me around.

Whistling and cheering echoes over the music, and I laugh deliriously, so overcome with joy. Warmth spreads through my body, to my soul.

"I love you, Mrs. Banner," he says when he slides me down his body, his hands going to my flat stomach.

"I love you more, husband," I whisper, before pulling his head down for a kiss, knowing every day, for the rest of my life, will be a happily ever after.

THE END

If you enjoyed Almost Free, please don't forget to leave a review. I enjoy reading your reviews, and I read ALL of them. They encourage me, motivate me, and help me know where I'm going right or wrong. Many readers choose to read a book recommended to them by a friend rather than from a Facebook post or ad, so if you liked the story, please do tell your friends on social media.

Next from Lisa Helen Gray is Aiden, and she has a surprise in store for you.

Author's Note

I'm going to keep this short and sweet and just say one big massive thank you to everyone for reading Almost Free.

Emma has been a WIP since I started writing Max's book. Her character screamed at me to write her, but she kept getting put to the back.

I am glad I waited. The story went in such a different direction than what it was originally set to. I'm proud of her story and how it turned out.

I've felt so much connection with Emma. I could relate to her. Seeing her shine and rise from the place she started was nothing short of awesome.

I really hope you enjoyed this book as much as I loved writing it.

And finally, Stephanie Farrant. I do not know what I would do without her. She's nothing short of amazing. The woman really knows how to make you feel better on a cloudy day and has become such a great friend through all of this.

Other Titles by Lisa Helen Gray

FORGIVEN SERIES

Better Left Forgotten

Obsession

Forgiven

CARTER BROTHERS SERIES

Malik

Mason

Myles

Evan

Max

Maverick

A NEXT GENERATION CARTER NOVEL SERIES

Faith

Aiden - Coming winter 2018

WHITHALL UNIVERSITY SERIES

Foul Play

Game Over - Out Now

Almost Free - Out now

I WISH SERIES

If I Could I'd Wish It All Away

Wishing For A Happily Ever After

Wishing For A Dream Come True - Coming Soon

About the Author

Lisa Helen Gray is Amazon's best-selling author of the Forgotten Series and the Carter Brothers series.

She loves hanging out, but most of all, curling up with a good book or watching movies. When she's not being a mum, she's a writer and a blogger.

She loves writing romance novels with a HEA and has a thing for alpha males.

I mean, who doesn't!

Just an ordinary girl surrounded by extraordinary books.

Printed in Poland
by Amazon Fulfillment
Poland Sp. z o.o., Wrocław